The Backwards House

Linda Hudson Hoagland

Linda Hudson Hoagland

ISBN: 1517794560

ISBN 13: 978-1517794569

DEDICATION

Michael E. Hudson

Matthew A. Hudson

Linda Hudson Hoagland

ACKNOWLEDGEMENTS

Publish America (America Star) of Baltimore for originally publishing this novel in 2009.

Victoria Fletcher, fellow author, for editing and formatting this book. She also developed the cover design for the book.

Linda Hudson Hoagland

CHAPTER 1: NEW NEIGHBORS

The little white house across the street from my home of five years stood empty for a very long time. The previous tenants had upped and moved out during the middle of the night for parts unknown. They weren't a friendly bunch and I didn't miss them. What I did miss was the safety in knowing I had a neighbor who was home at least part of the time. Not that I would have bothered that neighbor because I didn't and I wouldn't. It just felt safer to me to know that warm bodies occupied that house and, if push came to shove, I might be able to get help from them if I needed any help, that is.

I wasn't expecting any trouble nor was I expecting to need any help but a woman in her sixties, living all alone, well, you just never know, do you?

I didn't know to whom that house belonged. I guess I could have gone to the county courthouse to check it out if I really felt the need to do so. I assumed it was a rental because the inhabitants changed every few months.

I wasn't really a nosy busy body, but the house was located across the street and a little to the left of my front door. I couldn't avoid observing whether or not a car was parked outside or whether or not the blinds or draperies were opened. I didn't mean to spy. It was something I did naturally. I hoped my other neighbors watched my place with respect to noticing what looks out of the ordinary.

None of the people who had lived in that little white house had ever been friendly. Living in a small town, you would think that wouldn't have been true. Many times when I saw one of them outside, I would throw up my hand in a wave of hello or goodbye. It was never acknowledged by a nod or a glance and the wave was never returned.

"What was wrong with those people?" I mumbled as I watched the moving van crawl slowly up the street and stop in front of the little white house. "I hope the new people will, at least, wave."

Like I said, I'm not really a nosy busy body but I was interested in what the new neighbors looked like. I grabbed my big flower watering can, filled it to the brim with cold water, and walked out to my front porch. It was time to water my plants.

I tried to pour water into the flower pots while I surreptitiously stared from the corner of my eye at what was happening across the street. I didn't want to be too obvious about spying on the new neighbors. Actually I wasn't spying. I was curious, not spying.

I spent as much time as humanly possible watering the plants. I was sure the plants were all waterlogged and would probably drown before the day was over. But, what else could I do? I wanted a good view of what was being carried inside the house.

I went inside the house and peered through the front window as I stood behind the curtains so I could continue my neighbor watching.

The movers who were doing the lifting and hauling were all dressed in matching navy blue work uniforms with a large patch emblazoned across the back of the shirt saying "Diamond Movers" printed in blue letters against a white background. On the front, I could see a smaller patch over the left breast pocket that probably scripted the name of the wearer of the uniform.

There were four people doing the moving of goods. I think they were all men, but I can't be sure.   All of them appeared muscular and clean shaven. None of them displayed the attributes of day laborers. They went about their tasks quickly and efficiently.

When their job was completed, they closed all the blinds in the little white house and locked the front door before climbing back into the moving van and leaving the area.

The furniture looked brand new. Nothing looked worn and lived on like mine did. The cartons that were carried inside the house hid the contents from my prying eyes but I guessed that the merchandise contained within them was new, too.

"Who could afford to buy a whole house full of new furniture?" I asked my little dog, a Chihuahua named Nikki, as I stepped away from the front window. "Maybe they are newlyweds? That would be nice, wouldn't it, Nikki?"

I was talking to my dog again. I needed to get a life.

A couple of days passed that expended the weekend and there was no activity at the little white house across the street. I had hoped since the furniture had been moved to the house on Friday, while I was taking a vacation day from work, that the new occupants would have taken possession of the living quarters for the weekend. Then I would have been able to size up what I thought I might be able to expect from my new neighbors.

Monday morning my eyes glanced at the little white house across the street and saw no changes. There was no car parked in the driveway. The blinds remained closed to shut out the world. The occupants were unknown and not there.

I went to work with an air of disappointment exuding from my pores. My work hours seemed to drag on and on until four o'clock finally arrived. I rushed home hoping to continue my neighbor watching.

There was no change, no vehicles, and no opened blinds.

I started watching television after I completed my evening chores. I heard a car door bang.

I looked out my front window and saw a member of the Town of Stillwell Police Department walking onto the porch of the little white house across the street. I couldn't tell if it was an officer or the actual chief of police because his back was to me. He reached above the outside door where he felt around moving his hand searching for something for a few moments, and then he let himself inside the house.

"Nikki, maybe I'm going to have a town policeman living across the street from me. You certainly couldn't get any safer than that, could you?"

I was talking to the dog again.

I stood next to the front window waiting for the police officer to leave. I waited and waited. He seemed to be moving around inside the little house. He had flipped on the lights and I could see his dark shadowy form cross the blind covered windows every few seconds.

"He looks like he is straightening up and putting things away, Nikki. Maybe he is the one who is going to be living there."

I grew tired of standing next to the window so I tried to watch television again. I had no idea what was being displayed on my television screen. I had my ears attuned to the outside as I listened for new sounds.

I heard a car door again.

When I ran to the window I saw the police car driving away. The blinds were closed, the lights were off, and no one was in the little white house across the street.

My telephone rang.

"Are you the resident at 305 Valleyview Street?"

"Yes, why do you ask?"

"Just checking my records. Thank you."

The line was dead.

"Who was just checking? Who are you?" I asked the dead telephone.

Living alone, except for my little dog companion, made me somewhat paranoid. I didn't like the sound of that phone call.

Who was checking up on me? Why? I didn't harm anybody. I didn't get into anybody's personal business. I did look out my front window. I did watch the comings and goings at my neighbors' houses but I never carried tales. I spoke to no one about anything I had ever seen, at least, I hadn't to date. Maybe, maybe if I saw something that needed to be reported to the authorities, maybe I would do that. I would want the report to be anonymous, but I might report it, if I thought it was necessary. And, of course, there was Maggie, my neighbor and the closest thing to a best friend I had. I might tell her.

I hadn't seen anything going on anywhere that would warrant the telephone call with the exception of the moving van and the visiting police car.

Maybe I shouldn't be keeping an eye on the neighbors?

"Nikki, it's time to go to bed."

I went around my house locking and bolting every opening that someone might use to gain access to my domain. Just to make sure I would have no unwanted visitors, I placed a wooden chair back wedged beneath the doorknob for both the front and back doors. I carried the baseball bat to my bedroom where I laid it down on the floor next to my bed.

The baseball bat had been my front line of defense for many, many years. I wanted no gun in the house. I was afraid of guns. I was afraid I would use it if it found its way into my hand.

My sleep was restless and dream filled. Nikki had problems with sleeping also. She was up pacing the floor half the night.

I glanced at my clock with its bright red digital numbers lighting up the nightstand. It was four o'clock. I blinked my eyes searching for the reason I was awake.

I could hear the low growl emanating from my dog.

"What is it, girl? What's the matter?"

The growl continued low and vicious.

I reached for my robe and baseball bat.

I walked towards the growl.

"Where are you, girl?"

Suddenly the dog was barking loudly. Her tone was vicious and defensive. Never had I heard those ugly sounds coming from my tiny dog.

"Nikki, what is it? God, I wish you could talk. I wish you could answer me."

Nikki ran from room to room as if she were trying to catch someone or something on the other side of the walls, outside where the wee hours of the morning pointed out the fact that there should be no one walking anywhere around my house.

When Nikki reached the living room she stopped barking. The four o'clock visitor was gone.

I walked into the living room in my dark house. I had turned on no lights because I didn't want the person walking around outside to be able to figure out exactly where in my house I was at any moment. I sat in my easy chair with my baseball bat standing up next to me while I stroked my brave little dog.

There was to be no more sleeping.

After a couple of hours of sitting in the easy chair and stroking the dog, it was time to get ready for work. I was glad to have to get ready for the work day. I didn't know how much longer I was going to be able to sit and stroke Nikki as I waited for daylight.

****

"Sylvia, I think there was a prowler around my house around four o'clock this morning," I whispered to my coworker as soon as she arrived at the office we shared.

"A prowler? Why do you say that?"

"My little dog went crazy and I actually felt his prowler's presence?"

"How do you feel a prowler's presence?" she asked with her voice dripping in sarcasm.

"Whether you believe it or not, as the prowler made his way around the side of the house starting from the back, I watched my dog run from room to room following the prowler's noise trail that only she could hear. I knew when the prowler was gone because my internal radar told me it was safe."

"You didn't actually see anybody?"

"I didn't have to see anybody. My dog told me the prowler was there and my nerves verified it."

"Did you call the sheriff?"

"And tell him what?"

"What you told me."

"Did you believe me? Do you believe that I felt a prowler?"

"I see your point."

Sylvia paused trying to gather her thoughts.

"It's not that I don't believe you, Ellen, but feeling a prowler just isn't the same as seeing one."

"Yeah, sure."

"Did you check out your house?"

"What do you mean?"

"Did you go around to the back to see if the prowler did anything?"

"No, I never thought of that."

"Well, if I were you, I would check out the electrical box and the telephone connection box just to make sure there hasn't been any kind of wiretap or bomb attached to it."

"You're kidding me, aren't you?"

"Maybe about the bomb."

"That's encouraging."

"Just trying to help," she answered with a grin.

My mind worried about what she had said. A wiretap? A bomb? Why me? What did I do that was so bad?

"Sylvia, I also had a strange telephone call last night."

"What was so strange about it?"

"I never knew who called. The person, a man I think, on the other end asked if I was the resident at 305 Valleyview Street and, of course, I answered yes. It caught me off guard. I don't guess I should have said a word to him until he identified himself."

"Is that all he said?"

"That was it. He asked if I was the resident at 305 Valleyview Street. Why would he want to know that?"

"Maybe he wanted to check to see if he had the right telephone line; especially if they were placing a tap on the line."

"Why would anyone tap my line?"

"Have you done anything criminal, Ellen? Are you into dealing drugs? Prostitution? Money laundering?" she asked with a chuckle in her voice.

"Of course, I am, Sylvia. They are all my hobbies. I'm surprised you didn't know that."

"Well, there's your answer."

"All kidding aside, Sylvia, why would anyone be worried about me?"

"I don't have any idea."

The workday was busy and I didn't have time to do any more worrying until I arrived home.

"Nikki, come on, girl. Let's go outside and see what's what before it gets too dark."

Nikki and I exited the front door and slowly walked towards the back yard. I was looking for any evidence that the prowler might have left and Nikki had her nose to the ground checking out the scents.

The ground was semi soft from the recent rains and I hoped I would be able to see footprints left by the prowler who had mashed the grass down with his shoes. No such luck. Any grass that had been bent when he was walking around the house would have straightened itself right back up during the daylight hours while I was at work.

I continued my walk to the back where I located the electrical box and the telephone connection box. I stretched to my tip toes, being short was so aggravating at times, to reach the handle on the side of the electrical box so I could open it up and look inside. The handle was hard to pull down which led me to believe that the prowler hadn't touched the electrical box. When I looked inside I didn't know what I was looking for except that I hoped it wasn't a bomb.

Next was the telephone connection box. When I pulled on the cover of the box, it opened easily.

"Someone has been messing with this, Nikki."

Inside the box I saw a couple of clamps that I didn't remember ever seeing at any time in a telephone connection box.

"I think someone's listening in, Nikki. I need to get someone to look at this who knows what to look for," I told the dog as I closed the telephone connection box.

"Oh, God, I'm talking to the dog again," I said as I walked back to the front of my house.

"Come on, Nikki."

CHAPTER 2: SIC-EM, NIKKI!

With each passing day, I was getting more and more like my mother was before she died. I didn't like that, not one little bit.

The only friends I had in this little two-traffic light town were coworkers with the exception of my neighbor, Maggie. None of those coworkers were close enough to me to be labeled "best" or "good" friends; nevertheless, I felt fortunate to have them as friends.

I guess my lack of many close or best friends was my fault because I refused to be the odd woman out at any social functions. If the occasion called for an escort or date, I chose to stay home and brood about my single situation. If I could attend the function unescorted, I did; but, if the location of the event was several miles away from my home whether I could attend unescorted or not, I wouldn't go because I hated to drive, especially after dark.

It gave everyone who knew me the opinion that I was a loner. I guess I was - in a way.

The aloneness started after my husband died which was long after my two sons had moved away and started their own lives.

I really needed more close or best friends. I needed someone I could confide in and ask for advice, companionship, and most of all friendship. I wasn't husband shopping but the thought of having a man around the house was something I missed.

That's why I had a dog. I replaced my dead husband with Nikki. If only she could talk back to me. If only she could comfort me when I was scared. If only she could tell me what to do next.

I didn't get very many telephone calls so whoever was listening in was going to be disappointed.

My oldest son usually called me once a week. We talked more frequently because, even though he lived in the next town, it was still a local call.

My youngest son called about once a month when he remembered. If he forgot, I would call him so I could hear his voice. He lived so far away that I only got to see him about once every five years. He had visited two years earlier so I knew I wouldn't see his bright and smiling face for at least three more years. I wasn't going to drive to Nebraska to visit him and flying was totally out of the question with my income. I had thought of taking a Greyhound Bus to visit him in Nebraska but I would have to spend most of my vacation time sitting on the bus. Maybe after I retired I would do that bus trip.

"Nikki, what can we do, girl? Where do we go for help?"

I was thinking myself into a deep depression. I had to stop thinking about being alone. I had to stop wishing for my dead husband to walk through the door and sweep me off of my feet with his warm enveloping bear hug. I had to stop thinking about my two sons not living at home anymore.

I had to get a life.

A hobby, that's it! I needed a hobby that would take me out into the world where I might meet people in the same predicament that I was in which was alone, tee totally alone.

I had hobbies but they were the kind that did not require the aid or assistance of others. I crocheted, knitted, cross-stitched and did just about every kind of project that required a needle or hook.

My fourth grade teacher, Mrs. Smith, had taught me the rudiments of the knit stitch at school and I was self-taught from that point on. I could knit sweaters and anything else that I put my mind to do.

Crocheting was one of my two true hobbies. There wasn't anything that I couldn't make with a crochet hook and some time to spend on figuring out the pattern. I visited yard sales all summer long looking for the yarn I would need to make my multicolored afghans that I gave away at the drop of a hat. I gave afghans to people who were retiring from my office, or having babies, or having operations. No matter what the reason, they usually got an afghan.

Writing was my other true hobby. It definitely required no companionship in order to accomplish my goal.

My imagination was a big part of me and my life. If I thought about anything for a little while, I could always come up with a story, a tale of some kind, that I could make ring true.

As a child when attending school, I had the ability to write myself to an "A", but when I was given a choice for the answer, I would think myself into total confusion.

Was I doing that same thing about the little white house across the street? Was I making it into something it wasn't by building it up in my over eager mind?

Maybe----but so what?

"Nikki, let's go for a walk," I said to my little pooch as I reached for her leash.

The sound of the leash was pure delight for Nikki. She would bounce and jump around filled with excitement at the first sign of a walk.

My idea to take a walk was not an impulse move, it was something that I had firmly implanted in my mind from the moment I climbed out of bed and dressed for my workday.

I was going to go stand in front of the little white house across the street; and, at that same moment, Nikki would slip off of her leash and go running toward the little white house.

Nikki didn't want to cooperate. She wasn't interested in exploring the green, tall grass that filled the front yard of the little white house. I really could understand her hesitation. The grass towered over her tiny body.

"Go, Nikki," I whispered to her as I scratched the top of her head.

The little dog stood and looked at me, not making any effort at all to move.

"Go on, girl," I said as I motioned toward the little white house.

Nikki moved a step.

"Sic' em, Nikki," I said firmly.

Nikki took off running toward the little white house and didn't stop running until she reached the top step of what I considered the front porch; actually it was the back porch.

Of course, I had to go after my little runaway dog so I followed her up those very same steps. I picked up my little dog and held her snuggly against my chest as I casually walked to each window that faced the porch.

I looked through the window glass and saw heavy draperies blocking any kind of view to the inside of the house.

I knocked at the door facing the street for a few seconds and when no one answered, as I knew would be the case, I turned the doorknob to see if I could gain entry.

"Darn it!" I whispered softly when the doorknob wouldn't budge.

I placed Nikki down onto the porch and coaxed her down the steps.

I took a step toward the side of the house and whispered harshly to Nikki, "Sic' em, girl!"

Before long I was following my little runaway dog down the side of the little white house and ended up stopping dead in my tracks behind the little white house and completely out of view from the street.

"Nikki, where are you?" I whispered anxiously because I had lost sight of my precious pup.

I held my breath as I forced myself to be as quiet as I could. I heard no sounds of rustling weeds or tall grass or rapidly moving feet of any kind of animal.

"Nikki, come on, girl. Come to mama," I said as I strained my eyes to search for any movement in the dark recesses of the back yard.

I heard a low growling sound coming from behind me.

"Nikki, come here!" I shouted loudly very much afraid for me and my little dog.

The growling became louder and I took a tentative step towards the noise.

The grass rustled and my little dog burst from the tall grass and took a running leap into my arms.

She was so frightened her body was trembling as she tried to bury her face into my chest.

"Nikki, what's wrong?" I asked as I pulled her trembling body away from my chest so I could get a good look at her. "Did you see somebody? Did someone try to hurt my little girl?"

She writhed and wriggled around as I held her small body out in front of me so I could see her whole body.

"You're okay, girl. There's nothing on you that doesn't belong there," I said as I pulled her frightened body to me and covered her with my arms protecting her as much as I could from who knew what. "Let's get out of here, Nikki. I don't know what's going on in and around this little white house, but I don't think I really want to find out today, at least, not right now."

I held Nikki in my arms as I made my way across the street to the safety and protection of my own home. I didn't want to proceed with any more snooping into areas where I didn't belong. I vowed to myself that I would stop being so curious about people, places, and things that didn't concern me. I knew the vow was a waste of breath but I thought I would try.

I had no idea what had frightened Nikki to cause her to growl in such a serious tone. That was only the second time I had even heard that tone come from her small throat. But, whatever the reason for the serious growl, it was enough to scare both of us for the moment, at least until I could get my nerves settled so that I could move on.

I didn't like being scared off of my course by something I didn't understand. In other words, I was just plain outright nosy. I wanted to know what was going on and why they were being so secretive.

■■■

"Sylvia, do you know who moved into the little white house across the street from where I live?"

"Now, Ellen, how would I know who moved into that place?"

"I thought you might have heard some rumors. This is not a big city, you know. You can't flush your toilet twice without someone asking you why you're wasting water. You know how it is."

"Have you had any more funny phone calls?"

"No, but I'm expecting one any day now."

"Why? You haven't done anything to antagonize them have you?"

"Antagonize who?"

"You know, the person that threatened you?"

"Sylvia, I don't know who that person it."

"Oh, yeah. That's right. Well, then, you shouldn't have a problem."

"Oh, really? If I look out my front window, is someone going to blow my head off? And - what about the wiretap I think has been attached to my phone line? I'm afraid to say 'boo' over the telephone. I'm really beginning to pray that neither of my two sons calls. I'm afraid I might say something I shouldn't, then what will happen?"

"What are you going to do, Ellen?"

"I was hoping you might have an idea."

"No, nothing comes to mind except maybe you should sell out and move somewhere else?"

"No, I will not do that. As long as I have my health, I will keep my house. No matter what, I will keep my house."

"Okay, Ellen, I didn't mean to upset you."

"I know. I know. I'm sorry. I don't mean to take it out on you. It's been a long day and quitting time is finally here. I'm going to go home and see if my neighbor, Maggie, can offer me some new rumors from the neighborhood. She's retired and gets to talk to more people than I can ever think about talking to. Maybe she can tell me a thing or two."

"Okay, Ellen. See you tomorrow. Let me know what you come up with."

This game of Hide and Seek was getting a little too dangerous for my taste, I thought as I drove my Dodge

Neon through the light traffic headed for home and the happy sight of the welcome from Nikki.

I had always used the premise of Hide and Seek when I was trying to puzzle out my story lines and plots for my writing. I would pick something, an idea, a thought, that was hidden from my view and speculate on how I would find the answer to the puzzle. The seeking was the research, then hunting for an answer. It was a game. My own little life game that I played that involved no other participants except maybe a librarian or court clerk.

A game was supposed to be fun – not life threatening. A game should have participants with whom I enjoy the pleasure of sharing a laugh or two – not the solitary vigilance of constantly looking over my shoulder to see from what location the shoe was going to drop onto my head crushing my mere existence.

The so-called game I was playing was a question of survival.

CHAPTER 3: A BACKWARD HOUSE

"Who moved into the little white house across the street?" I asked my neighbor, Maggie, as we both walked to our mail boxes that stood side by side in front of our houses.

"I don't know who they are. They are awful secretive about their comings and goings. They actually moved into the place in the middle of the night."

"No, they moved the furniture and a bunch of boxes in one evening before dark."

"Well, I saw them move in some clothes on hangers and a bunch of boxes a few nights ago," said Maggie in a conspiratorial whisper as she glanced toward the little white house that stood with its backside facing the street.

"Did you get a good look?"

"No, I really couldn't tell the gender of any of them but I saw four people."

"Why was that house built backwards on this street?"

"Someone told me that the man who built it many years ago was angry with somebody who lived on the same street so when he had his house constructed he didn't want his home facing that same somebody."

"That sounds really stupid," I commented.

"It does, doesn't it? How did you know those people moved in at night?"

"I saw them back the truck up to the door. I'm surprised you didn't hear it. They sure caused a lot of racket."

"Did you see any of them, the ones who live there, I mean?"

"I'm not sure. I saw four different people unloading the truck, I think they were all men, but I don't know if any of them were the new neighbors or just the movers. They seemed to be in a hurry when they were unloading the truck. I was watching them for a while and they were practically running back and forth carrying all those clothes and lots of boxes. Oh yeah - I also saw a police officer."

"Who was it?"

"I don't know. All I could see was his backside adorned in a uniform."

"Are you sure it was a 'he'?"

"No."

"Was anybody home when the police officer arrived?"

"No, he found a key hidden above the front or back door."

"Really? It's a shame you didn't know about the key. You would have paid the house a visit."

"Yeah! Right! I've seen a dark-haired woman go into the house at eleven o'clock at night," I whispered. "It was too dark to really get a good look."

"Well, I think I saw a man with brown hair leave at about five in the morning. He looked like he was trying to sneak out without making any noise."

"How could you tell he was sneaking?"

"He kept his head down and his shoulders hunched over most of the time except when he was checking to see if anyone was coming down the street. That's when I got a look at him. It was like he could tell he was being watched. I know he didn't see me but he kept looking up and down the street."

"Did you get a good look at his face?"

"No, it was still too dark. Listen! I think I hear my phone ringing. I'll call you later. Tell me if you find out anything new," said Maggie as she started running towards her front door.

My curiosity was getting aroused to the point that I had to continue to play my game of Hide and Seek with the little white house across the street as the centerpiece. My method of playing the game was a little different. I didn't play the game in the traditional manner of looking for the person or persons in a short period of time that were told to go hide from sight.

My game of Hide and Seek consisted of my seeking the information the people in the small white house across the street were trying to hide from me no matter how much of my time was used.

I called Maggie to ask more questions.

"Maggie, didn't that house used to belong to the church that's standing next to it?"

"Yeah, but I think the church sold it about a year or so ago."

"Who to?"

"I don't know."

"I'll call you later. I'm going to the courthouse on my lunch hour tomorrow to check on a deed. I'll tell you if and when I find out anything."

As a purchase order clerk for the local school system, I worked at the Central Office where I could slip off, on occasion, to do a little side trip or investigation of my own. If I were a secretary in a school, that little trick wouldn't be possible.

My job prior to becoming an employee for the county was as a legal assistant/secretary for a local attorney. I knew a thing or two about looking up records at the courthouse.

I was on a mission. I was pursuing the next step of my Hide and Seek game.

Paging though transfers of real estate proved fruitful when I found the deed that transferred the little white house to a Jonathan Smith of Alexandria, Virginia. My thought was that they could have picked a better name. Jonathan Smith? Really?

The real estate transfer happened over a year earlier but I was sure no Jonathan Smith ever lived in that little white house during that period of time.

"Sounds like a phony name to me," I mumbled as I requested and paid for a copy of the deed.

I had to leave my game as it stood for the moment and discontinue the paper chase because my lunch hour had already come to an end. As a matter of fact, I was going to be late getting back to the office, as if it mattered to anyone but me. I take that back, it does matter to those who stand at the door with a stop watch in hand not taking into account all of the times I hauled work home with me without charging them a penny of overtime. I don't do that anymore. Or, at least, I try not to but sometimes the pressure gets to me and I cave in again and haul the work home without the knowledge of the powers that be.

■■

"Maggie, did you ever hear of a Jonathan Smith living around here?"

"No, is that who is supposed to be the person living there?"

"The deed is in his name."

"Did the deed say where he is from?" probed Maggie.

"Alexandria, Virginia. Why would anyone living in Alexandria want to buy a house clear across the state in Stillwell County, Virginia?"

31

"Good question. Maybe it's a real estate investment."

"A backward house in this small town? He's not much of an investor."

"No, I guess not."

"I wonder if he bought it so he could hide something or someone."

"Could be. But why here?"

"Would you look for anything valuable or anybody famous in this small wide spot on the road to nowhere?"

"Ellen, that's a terrible way to describe our little town."

"It's true, Maggie. You know it's true. All of the kids have to leave to find jobs. They have to go where the industry and the money is."

"Maybe so but that's still a terrible thing to say."

"Alexandria is up around Washington, D.C., isn't it?" I asked as I tried to steer the conversation into a new direction.

"So?"

"Maybe the brown-haired man and dark-haired woman are spies?"

"Ellen, your writer's imagination is running away from you?" scolded Maggie.

"Could be, you know. Sometimes the spies have to go underground for one reason or another."

I watched the little white house across the street every chance I could get. I would extinguish all of the lights in my house and sit next to my window watching any and all of the activity in that little white house.

The telephone was ringing. It was eleven o'clock at night. No one should be calling me this late unless it was an emergency. I picked up the receiver and held it next to my ear for a moment. I was expecting the call to be an obscene one.

"Ellen Holcombe?"

"Yes, may I help you?'

"Don't be watching that house across the street from you anymore. Don't be checking on records at the courthouse or asking any more questions of any one about that house. Do you understand?"

"Why?" was all I could say.

"You've been warned."

"Warned about what?"

The telephone line was dead.

I pressed star 69 to see where the call originated but nothing happened.

I went to bed to try to get some sleep, but all I could do was toss and turn. I kept wondering what was going on in that little white house.

****

"Maggie, someone threatened me, again, last night," I whispered into the telephone as soon as I arrived home from what seemed to be the longest work day of my life after tossing and turning all night. "Oh, jeez," I said as I realized that my phone could be bugged or tapped. "Meet me out back, now."

"What happened? Who threatened you?" asked an excited Maggie.

"That man told me not to watch the little white house across the street or go to the courthouse to do any more checking. How did he know about that?"

"What man? I don't know how he knew. Maybe he saw you sitting in front of your window or he could have followed you when you went to the courthouse."

"Yeah, did you get any phone calls? You've been watching them, too."

"No, none."

"I don't know who he is. I don't know who called me. I think he has tapped my phone and most likely he checked the records at the courthouse because I had to pay for the deed copy."

"Are you going to do what he said?"

"What do you think?"

"No, you're going to keep on snooping until you get yourself killed."

"I'm going to the courthouse tomorrow to see who is paying the property taxes. You want to meet me there?"

"No, I don't think so."

"Maggie, they are not going to scare me off my game. I'll find some answers."

"Be careful, this game of Hide and Seek could be dangerous."

Nikki was nervous, too nervous for my liking. She would react to every sound as if it were as loud as thunder and as shocking as the brightest lightning on the darkest night.

"What's the matter, girl?" I asked her as I tried to soothe her with my hand gliding down her tiny backside.

Nikki's actions were beginning to affect me. I would jump at the slightest noise or flash of light.

"Girl, we've got to stop acting like this," I said boldly as I walked to the front door trying to appear casual as I checked on the little white house across the street. "There's no one there, Nikki. Neither one of us should be afraid."

It was early morning and the only flashing lights were the scene changes on the television screen that was broadcasting the morning news. Even though I knew I shouldn't be nervous and afraid, I couldn't convince my brain to accept the truth.

I was glad it was a work day. I had to focus on something other than fear, which seemed to be completely taking over my every waking moment. I believed Nikki sensed my feelings and she was displaying her own form of fear.

"Nikki, I'm getting ready for work and, today, you're going with me. You're too upset and nervous to be left here all alone," I said to my little dog as she looked at me with her pleading dark brown eyes.

I swear, I think she understood what I said because she waited until I made my bed, then quickly jumped up on it so she could watch me dress for my workday. She seemed almost to be smiling.

"Maybe Maggie was right, Nikki. I'm letting my writer's imagination run away with me," I said as I held my beloved dog close to my heart as I made my way out of my front door toward my car that was parked in my driveway.

I took my little dog and her favorite blanket into my office. It was my hope that Nikki would not be a disturbance to those who were present on the second floor. I expected her to stay put and not be a bother, which is exactly what she did. I guess she was as happy to be away from the worry as I was.

At the end of the day, Nikki and I went home. That used to be something I looked forward to doing, but now, I was afraid.

What bothered me most about my fear was that I wasn't sure what I was afraid of or who? Nothing specific had been said, no descriptions of what had happened or what was going to happen came my way. I was warned to do no more investigating, but he didn't say what would happen if I continued.

Was he going to kill me?

Was he going to burn my house down with me in it?

For that matter, who is "he"? Was it a "he"?

Why would he even care what an older woman nearing retirement age would do?

Why were there strange additions to my telephone connection box?

Who did it and, especially, why?

CHAPTER 4: IMMACULATE MAGGIE

I tried to call Maggie, but there was no answer. I wanted to talk to someone who could commiserate with me about my predicament, if I had a predicament.

What if it was my writer's imagination?

No – no – that can't be true. I was warned. It's not all my imagination.

"Nikki, let's go look at that telephone connection box again. What with all of the new-fangled gadgets they have now-a-days, I really don't understand why they would need to wiretap my telephone the old-fashioned way."

Again, I was talking to my dog. I had no one else, so she was the chosen one to hear my out loud conversations. Sometimes I had to say the words out loud to get the meaning of what I was trying to tell myself.

"Let's walk over to Maggie's house, since no one is home, and look at her telephone connection box, if I can find it and hopefully reach it."

My ever attentive Nikki wanted me to carry her. She was so spoiled, but I had no one to blame but myself.

I started looking on the side of Maggie's house that was closest to my house. I couldn't remember seeing it on that side but, then again, I hadn't been looking for it until now.

"It's not here, Nikki. Let's go to the other side."

I walked around the front of the house noticing that the blinds were closed as if Maggie hadn't opened them that morning or perhaps she had closed them early anticipating a late return from where ever she went.

There was no sign of the telephone connection box in the front of the house or on the side farthest from my home. That left only the back of the house and I wasn't too keen on looking there because it was starting to get dark.

"Let's look really fast, Nikki. I hate to be prowling around someone's house after dark."

My little dog started to tremble as I held her in my arms. "This won't take long, girl."

I increased my walking pace and hurried around the corner expecting to see a dark area between the house and an out building that would not be very inviting. Much to my surprise, it wasn't dark. The outside light was shining brightly lighting up the entire space permitting me to see that no one was skulking behind the house waiting to attack at the first sign of movement.

"Nikki, Maggie left the light on. I wonder why she did that. It's so unlike her to leave the back light shining. She does leave the front porch light on most of the time for whatever reason; but, why the back light?"

I spotted the telephone connection box a little to the left of the back door. As I walked toward the box, I noticed that Maggie's back door was standing open. I tugged at the storm door and it was unlocked.

"Maggie? Maggie? Are you here?" I shouted as fear flushed through my body.

I placed Nikki on the floor as I entered the house when I received no response to my shouts.

"Go find Maggie, Nikki," I said as I pushed her forward with my hand.

Nikki wouldn't move. She stood statue still and whimpered.

"You are such a chicken for a dog," I said in disgust as I started walking slowly into the kitchen.

Everything looked fine. Nothing was out of place like it would be in my house. Maggie kept her house spotless and shining. I, on the other hand, lived in my house, not for my house.

Nikki wasn't going to move without help so I snatched her tiny body up from the floor. I held her with my left arm and hand against my body while with my right hand, I grabbed the hammer that I knew was in the cabinet drawer nearest to the door.

Nikki must have felt my fear because her trembling became more obvious as she tried to hide her face from whatever she thought was lying in wait for the two of us.

I'm not a tiny woman. I'm short and I have more girth than I care to admit, made even wider, as I clutched Nikki and held a hammer at the ready. Sneaking was out of the question.

"Maggie, are you here?" I whispered.

Silence.

"I'm coming into the dining room now," I said as an announcement to anyone who might be lying in wait.

I entered the dining room. I used the hammer to push the light switch to illuminate the dark corners.

Nothing – no Maggie. Nothing was out of place except there was still no Maggie to be seen.

"Maggie, please answer me. Where are you? Are you sick? Are you hurt?" I whispered softly as I continued my search for my best friend and neighbor, Maggie Boothe.

I moved on to the living room where I saw a coffee cup almost full sitting on the coffee table. Maggie must have been watching television, probably the morning news, when she took the notion to leave.

Immaculate Maggie would not have left the coffee cup on the table if she were given a choice. That was the first sign that Maggie was missing. She wouldn't have left the cup of coffee just sitting there. There must have been an emergency that caused her to leave in a really big hurry.

I placed Nikki on Maggie's sofa so I could get a stronger grip on the hammer. I felt I needed a two-handed hold on it before I proceeded to the bedrooms.

"Nikki, stay right there. Okay, girl? I don't want you in the way or getting hurt," I said as I tried to comfort my frightened dog.

I could have used some comforting, too. I was scared to death.

The house, Maggie's house, was so eerily quiet. The sounds of my own breathing were deafening.

With a better two-handed grip on the handle, I started walking slowly down the hall that led to the bedrooms. As I progressed into each room, I had flicked the light switch to illuminate all areas. I left the lights on in each room as I progressed to another.

Not having found Maggie lying in a puddle of blood in the kitchen, the dining room, or living room, I was afraid I would uncover a bloody, gruesome scene in her bedroom.

"Maggie, please be okay," I prayed.

Maggie's house was not big. It had the three rooms I've already mentioned along with three bedrooms and one centralized bathroom. It was an older house, about thirty years old, but well cared for by Maggie who had owned it for twenty of those thirty years.

My house, on the other hand, was only six years old. It was built in almost the same layout as Maggie's house by Stillwell County Habitat for Humanity.

My husband and I were lucky enough to get the house after the previous occupant got married and moved herself and her children into a new home purchased by her new husband.

My husband passed away about eight years after we moved into the Habitat House and I have made it my goal in life to honor my commitment by paying for my house. Without Habitat's help, I wouldn't have ever owned my own home. Now, I didn't intend to let them down by not making my monthly house payments.

"Maggie, where are you? Please be alive," I whispered in prayer.

The bedroom door was closed. That was odd, Maggie usually let the doors stand open.

I walked close to the door where I strained with all of my might to hear any sounds from within the room. I held my breath to prevent my own internal noises. I leaned forward placing my ear against the door.

Nothing – nada – no sounds.

What did I want? Was I looking to find Maggie gasping a final breath? If she were alive, I would have heard something by now, wouldn't I?

I reached for the doorknob turning it slowly.

"Stop it?" I told myself. "There's no one in there. Quit acting like a fool." Sometimes it took a full-fledged personal conversation with myself to get me focused.

I opened the door quickly, pushing it to the side, and reached for the light switch. I wanted no shadows in the room whatsoever.

The loud click of the light switch produced no illumination.

Suddenly I felt something cold against my ankle and I screamed. I jumped away from the feeling of cold and further into the dark room.

"Who's there?" I whispered harshly.

I looked toward the light in the hall filtering in from the living room and saw my frightened little dog running as fast as she could as she searched for a place to hide.

"Nikki, come here, girl," I shouted when I realized it had been Nikki's cold nose that caused me to jump. "Come on, girl. I'm sorry I jumped and scared you."

I walked into the living room and found her cowering on the sofa shaking from head to all four sets of toes. I picked her up into my arms. I held her body against mine with my left arm and placed the hammer in my left hand. I needed a flashlight that I located in the kitchen. I switched the flashlight to my left hand as I held the hammer, again, with my right hand. It was awkward, but it would have to do.

I walked toward the dark bedroom.

There was no smell of death in the house. That was something for which I was truly grateful.

"Let's get this over with, Nikki. My poor nerves can't handle much more."

I shined the flashlight around the dark bedroom but found nothing in disarray. I was disappointed. I was ashamed of myself for being disappointed.

"Just a plain, ordinary burnt out light bulb, Nikki. That's all there is to it. Let's check the other two bedrooms and the bathroom and get out of here."

Nikki licked my arm. I knew she understood me.

Nothing was disturbed in the two remaining bedrooms and the bathroom was spotless, as usual. I back tracked my steps through each room returning them to darkness and flipped the lock as I went out the back door. Before I closed the door, I remembered I hadn't checked the telephone answering machine. I raced back into the house in the semi darkness and pressed the play button next to the flashing light that indicated there were stored messages waiting to be heard.

"Mom, call me when you get home. Not an emergency. Just want to talk."

I smiled at that message. I get them like that sometimes.

"Mrs. Boothe, this is Dr. Jacobson's Office. I'm calling to remind you of your appointment tomorrow at one o'clock."

"I hope Maggie's not sick, Nikki."

"Mrs. Boothe."

There was a long pause filled with the very faint sounds of a different conversation in the background.

"Mrs. Boothe, I know you're there."

That caught my undivided attention.

"Mrs. Boothe, pick up the phone, now."

I heard the click of the answering machine being turned off. Then – nothing.

"Oh, my God, Nikki. Something's wrong, bad wrong." I turned to leave again when another thought crossed my mind. "Let's look in the fridge, girl."

Inside the refrigerator was a note addressed to me.

Ellen,

I got a call from someone who says he knows my son telling me to meet him out on Route 460 at a flea market set up in front of the skating rink. He sounded mad and upset about something and I'm really worried about what he might do. This problem goes back a couple of years and I thought everything had been settled. I knew you would find the note no matter where I put it. I should be back by tonight. If not, call the police.

Love,

Maggie

I stared at the note. According to the piece of paper I held in my hand, Maggie should be here – now. The note was dated yesterday and last night was when she should have returned.

I carried the note and my dog out of the back door that I made sure was unlocked. I wanted to be able to get in the house when I brought the police back with me.

I stopped in front of Maggie's telephone connection box and stared at it for a moment. Rather than open it and leave my fingerprints while obliterating someone else's fingerprints, I decided to wait until the police got there. They could check her box and mine to see if there were problems with the inside workings of either box.

Nikki and I went home to call 9-1-1.

CHAPTER 5: FRESH BLOOD

My best friend, Maggie Boothe, was missing and I wanted her back safe and sound in her own little house right next door to mine.

Rather than call the police, I decided to visit the police station and report the problem in person.

"I want to report someone missing."

"How long?"

"What?"

"How long has that person been missing?"

"I'm not sure. At least twenty-four hours, maybe longer."

"That's not long enough."

"What?"

"You can't report a missing person after only twenty-four hours."

"There is a note. I have it here. It says to call the police if she didn't get home."

"What's your name?"

"My name is Ellen Holcombe. The person missing is Maggie Boothe."

"How long did you say she was missing?"

"I'm not sure exactly. Look at this note, please."

I thrust the note at the police officer who appeared not to be interested in the topic at hand. It was my intention to get him interested one way or another.

The startled police officer looked at the note and became a little more interested.

"Where did you get this note?"

"In Maggie's refrigerator."

"In her refrigerator? Why would she leave you a note in her refrigerator?"

"I don't know, but that's where I found it. Maybe she didn't want anyone else to find it. Would you look in the refrigerator for a note?"

"No ma'am, I wouldn't. Why did you?"

"I don't know. I just did, that's all. Are you going to help me find her?"

"This Maggie Boothe is a close friend?"

"My best friend. I know she's in trouble. The note says so. Are you going to help me or not?"

"We need some more information first, ma'am."

"Fine, what else do you need to know?" I asked as I was getting totally frustrated with the conversation. Maggie could be dead and buried before this man could get it through his head that I needed help in finding her. He wasn't asking the important questions. It wouldn't have mattered if he did. I didn't have any answers.

"This note doesn't say who she was going to meet? Do you know?"

"No sir, I don't have any idea."

"Maybe she took a few days to renew an old friendship."

"I don't think so. The letter doesn't seem to indicate to me that she wanted to renew the relationship."

"Is there a Mr. Boothe?"

"I believe he is dead. She never talks about him so I assume he is dead."

"You don't know that for sure?"

"No sir, I don't."

Finally he started filling out a form so that information could, at least, be placed in a file. I answered everything that I could. I even gave the officer the name and address of Maggie's son so he could be called and scared to death about his missing mother.

"Do you have a key to Mrs. Boothe's house?"

"No sir. She left the back door unlocked so that I could get in and find the note."

"Does she usually leave the back door unlocked?"

"No, never."

"Why did you check the door?"

"She left the back light shining and I thought that was peculiar since I knew she wasn't home because I had tried to call her earlier."

"Why would you think there was any kind of a problem?"

"Well, that's because of some strange happenings that have been going on around me. That's a whole different story. I don't want to get into that now. I want to find Maggie."

"Do you know of any threats that Mrs. Boothe may have received?"

"No, not Maggie."

"Have you received any threats?"

"Why would you ask that?"

"Because of the way you answered my question about Mrs. Boothe and threats. Have you received any threats?"

"Yes sir, I have. I don't understand why, but I have."

"Tell me about them."

"It was just a phone call. The person called it a warning. I don't know who it was or why he called. Now, please help me find Maggie. I left the back door of her house unlocked. Follow me and I will lead you to her house and take you inside where you will see that nothing looks out of place or disturbed except a coffee cup sitting on the coffee table in the living room."

"A coffee cup and this note. That's all you have?"

"Yes sir. That's all I need to have to know that Maggie needs help."

I was begging at this point. Tears were pooling up in my eyes. I reached for my handbag and rifled the contents searching for a tissue so I could stem the flow of the tears that were teetering on the edge of my eyelids.

"Is this the correct address for Mrs. Boothe?"

"Yes."

"As soon as another officer arrives to take my place here in this office, I will drive over there to check it out. You live next door on the right or left?"

"Right."

"I'll check in with you first so you'll know I'm there. I wouldn't want you to think I was a burglar or something worse."

"That would be good because I wouldn't want to have to hit you over the head with my cast iron frying pan," I said with a smile. It was my first attempt to smile since I had walked into the police station.

I left the police station and headed for home again.

Nikki greeted me at the door with the enthusiasm of welcoming a long awaited special surprise guest. I probably should have taken her with me when I visited the

51

police station but I would make it up to her by giving her a little extra loving attention.

Even though Nikki was only a dog, she was my dog, my friend, and my companion. I wanted to make her happy and keep her happy any way that I could. I needed Nikki because I needed someone or something to care for since the passing of my husband. Nikki fit the bill perfectly. I wasn't sure if I wanted to replace her with another man or not. Until I made that decision, if I ever made that decision, Nikki was a big part of my home life.

I paced the floor waiting for the police officer to make an appearance.

The telephone interrupted my worry about Maggie with its loud, insistent ring. I lunged at the noise, grasping it, hoping it was the police officer telling me he found Maggie.

"Hello," I shouted breathlessly.

"Mrs. Holcombe? Are you Mrs. Holcombe?"

"Yes, I am. Who are you?" I asked apprehensively.

"I'm Agent Thompson with the Federal Bureau of Investigation."

"The FBI? Why would the FBI want to talk with me? Is this about Maggie Boothe? Has she been kidnapped?" I asked excitedly as my mind raced through the many possible scenarios that might involve Maggie.

"Ma'am, I'm calling about an investigation we are conducting concerning the inhabitants of the white house located across the street from you."

I looked out my window. I had a feeling this man was calling me from a phone where he could see me.

"What about them?" I wasn't sure I wanted to talk to this person over the phone lines. I wanted to see some proof that he was FBI.

"Mrs. Holcombe, we would like to ask you these questions in person, if you don't mind?"

"I would prefer the face to face myself."

"Would tomorrow morning at ten o'clock be good?"

"No, I have to work."

"What about five o'clock tomorrow afternoon?"

"That would be fine. But tell me, why are you asking questions about an empty house? No one lives there, you know."

"We will see you tomorrow afternoon, Mrs. Holcombe."

The phone line was silent. I continued holding the receiver to my ear. I wanted to listen for any telltale signs of an intruder horning in on my conversations.

There was a clicking sound and then the silence was replaced with a jarring dial tone. The clicking sound, was that normal? I didn't have a clue.

"Nikki, I wish Maggie was home. I really need someone to talk to," I said as I cradled my dog in my arms. "I know what I can do, girl. I've got to find the phone book. I want to look up the telephone number for the FBI. I'll ask for Agent Thompson. I think that's what he said his name was."

I continued to hold Nikki while I walked around the house as I looked for the telephone book that I never seemed to be able to put back into the same place twice.

"There it is," I said as I grabbed it and placed it on the kitchen table. With one hand I paged through the white pages to locate the Federal Bureau of Investigation. Nothing listed in the white pages so I turned to the area marked by the blue pages representing all forms of government from local to federal. Nothing, no FBI, but there was a listing for the Secret Service. Thanks, but no thanks.

I flipped to the first page of the phone book and found it listed under Other Important Numbers. I was sure glad it wasn't an emergency.

There were two listings in cities that were both over a hundred miles away with a third number located over four hundred miles from my home.

I called Bristol first.

"Do you have an Agent Thompson working out of your office?"

"Your name, please?"

"I'm Ellen Holcombe and I received a phone call from a man who said he was an FBI Agent. I just want to verify that he is. Do you have an Agent Thompson?" I asked firmly trying to indicate that I meant business.

"No ma'am, we have no Agent Thompson in this office."

"Thanks," I said as I hung up the receiver to disconnect the line.

I called Roanoke to check with that office.

"Do you have an Agent Thompson?" I asked as, once again, I explained the purpose of my call.

"Do you have a first name for this Agent Thompson?"

"No, he didn't tell me his first name."

"It was a man? You're sure it was a man?"

"Yes, I am."

"We don't have a male agent with the name of Thompson."

"Do you have a female Thompson?"

"Yes ma'am."

"Does she have a husky voice?"

"No, she doesn't. She has a high timbered voice with very much of a female sound to it."

"Thanks anyway for your help," I said as I looked for the Richmond telephone number.

After two rings the line was answered.

"Agent Thompson, please."

"I'm sorry he's not here right now. Could someone else help you?"

"No, you've already answered my question. Bye," I whispered as I hung up the receiver and was a little relieved. At least, I knew there was a male Agent Thompson working for the FBI out of the Richmond Office.

"Nikki, let's go for a ride."

I grabbed my handbag and headed for the front door carrying my dog. At that moment, I decided it was extremely important to go to the grocery store. Actually, I just wanted to get out of the house for a few minutes because my nerves were bothering me.

I climbed onto the front seat when I noticed the police officer pull into Maggie's driveway. The officer seemed to be sitting and watching Maggie's house for any signs of movement.

I decided to do the same except that I was watching the police officer.

Finally, I had enough of watching the officer do nothing. I exited my car and walked across both front yards with Nikki close on my heels.

"Sir, did you need to see me?" I shouted when I was a few feet from his vehicle.

He nodded and started moving around, pushing this button, and flipping a switch or two.

"Mrs. Holcombe, are you going somewhere?"

"I was going to the grocery store, but that can wait. Finding Maggie is more important. Follow me and I'll show you where you can get into her house," I said trying to urge him along his way.

"Did you re-enter the house after speaking with me at the police station?"

"No sir, I did not. Is there a problem?"

"I don't know, not yet, anyway. Just checking before I go inside."

"Oh, okay," I said as I tried to figure out what his problem was about Maggie's house.

The police officer stood by the back door with his hand on the door handle of the storm door.

"I don't like doing this without a piece of paper saying it's all right. I guess I'll have to make an exception this time."

"I'll go inside with you, Officer. The note was addressed to me and I did as the note instructed. I'll take the blame if there is any to be handed out."

As soon as we walked inside, I could see that the kitchen was not as I had left it.

"I thought you said nothing was out of place?"

"I did say that. All of this has happened since I talked to you earlier today. It might have been done when I was at your office because I have seen no one come or go since I got home. Look at the mess? Maggie will be so upset. Why would anybody do this? Maggie never hurt anybody," I said as I tried to hold back the tears of anger and frustration that were trying to burst forth.

"Take a look around here and I'll check out the rest of the house to be on the safe side."

"Sure, no problem."

"And don't touch anything if you can avoid doing so. If you must touch something, cover your fingertips with a towel."

"Yeah," I said as I shook my head in disgust.

I wanted to pick up everything that was on the floor and put it back into place, but I didn't.

Drawers had been pulled out of the cabinet frames and the contents had been emptied onto the floor. Whoever did this was searching for something. That was obvious from the items being stirred around and separated from the other items that had been in the same drawer.

In one of the drawers I noticed a newspaper clipping about a bank robbery that had happened a couple of months earlier.

"Why would Maggie keep this?" I asked myself as I turned to the opposite side of the article and saw only advertising information for a florist shop. I shoved the newspaper article into my pocket. I would take more time with it later.

"The rest of the house looks just like the kitchen. It's a real mess. I don't think a vandal did this because most of it isn't broken. Someone was searching for something. Do you have any idea of what that could be?"

"No, Officer, no idea. Maggie is a retired school teacher. What in the world could she have done to upset someone so much? What could she be hiding?"

"You're sure you know nothing about why this has happened?"

"What are you trying to say, Officer?"

"Well, you said you were best friends. Maybe you're trying to keep a secret to help protect Maggie's good name."

"If I knew anything, I would tell you. So help me God, I would tell you everything if it would help me find Maggie."

"Use these rubber gloves and help me find the phone. Maybe there is a message on it that could help us."

"I'll play the message I heard earlier today."

"What did it say?"

"It called out her name telling her to pick up the phone. The voice was not pleasant. It sounded like the person was putting forth an effort to hold a controlled conversation, if you know what I mean."

"What else did the voice say?"

"Nothing, just pick up the phone, now. Then I heard the click of the answering machine being turned off."

Was it a man or a woman?"

"I think it was a man. The voice sounded too heavy to be a woman."

"Did you recognize the voice?"

"No."

"Where is the answering machine usually hooked up? What room?"

"In the living room."

"I don't see it. Do you?"

"No, they must have taken it with them?

"Looks that way."

"What do we do now?" I asked as I pondered the hope that I could help.

"Nothing, at the moment. I'll get a team over here to check for prints. Until then, nothing can be done."

"Can't you get a list of phone calls made to her number?"

"Sure, but I'll have to do that at the office. You should go on home. Maybe your friend will try to contact you. If she does, call me right away."

"Okay. There's nothing I can do?"

"No ma'am. I'll go to my car and get the investigation team notified using my radio. Then I'll wait until they show up."

"Do you drink coffee, Officer?"

"Yes, I do. Call me Barry, Barry Johnson, not Officer. It seems like we're going to become friends," he said as he smiled broadly below the trimmed graying mustache on his upper lip.

"Barry, you'll end up being my best friend if you help me find Maggie. I'll bring you some coffee out to your car. Cream or sugar?"

"Neither, black is fine."

"A man after my own heart," I mumbled as I left Maggie's house.

Nikki was waiting for me outside the door and greeted me with much love and licking.

"I think he's actually going to help, Nikki. We'll find Maggie safe and sound. I know we will, girl."

As fresh coffee was brewing, I walked into the living room to check on the house across the street. It looked like no one was home, but you really couldn't tell too much about it in the day time because no lights were shining.

The little white house across the street seemed to be calling to me, beckoning me to enter through its threshold to the secrets within its walls.

There had been no activity around the little white house for days. That is, no activity from other people excluding Nikki and me, of course.

The backside of the little white house that faced my front door seemed to be making fun of me, mimicking me, with its smiling, smirking mouth of a door, and dark glistening windows that were the two eyes watching my every move.

I knew it was my imagination that was plaguing me to my very soul. The unknown, the secrets that were lurking on the other side of the street, taunted me.

Barry, the Police Officer, sat in his car in Maggie's driveway for almost an hour before the crime investigation team made an appearance. I carried coffee to him twice and allowed him the use of my bathroom facilities once, much to the disdain of Nikki who didn't want to share any part of her happy home with a stranger.

I did not proceed with my trip to the grocery store that had been put on hold hours earlier. I was too interested in watching the comings and goings at Maggie's house to miss one single moment of observation.

Barry, the Police Officer, stayed close to Maggie's house the entire time that the strangers were sifting through it looking for clues.

The house had been cordoned off with yellow police tape and the strangers had packed up and left the neighborhood when Barry knocked on my front door.

"Mrs. Holcombe?" he said loudly.

"Yes, Officer-e-r-r, Barry. What can I do for you?"

"I need to ask you a few more questions."

"Sure, come on in. Did they find anything that would help locate Maggie?"

"We're not sure, not until we run some tests."

"What kind of tests?"

"Fingerprints, blood, etc. You know. Everything you see on TV."

"Blood? You found blood?"

"Yes, in the bedroom. Quite a bit of it actually."

"I didn't see any blood when I walked through the house the first time. I wasn't looking for blood the second time. I thought someone had just ransacked the place looking for something to steal."

"You didn't see any blood before all the destruction?"

"No, not a bit," I answered as I struggled to hold back the tears that were rushing forward.

"Well, it probably isn't Mrs. Boothe's blood if you didn't see it on your walk through the first time," said the deputy as he tried to quell my fears.

"How do you know it's not Maggie's blood?" I demanded.

"We don't. I was trying to be encouraging."

"Thanks, Barry, but my mind always jumps to the worst scenario because I've become a cynic over the many years I've spent trying to survive."

"I know what you mean."

"Do you? I wonder," I whispered under my breath.

"What else did you need to know?" I asked.

"Maggie Boothe has how many children?"

"One son."

"Do you have a phone number and address for him?'

"I gave it to the officer that took the information at the police station. Her son's name is Marty, Martin Boothe. He should be listed in the phone book. He lives somewhere out on Cumberland Road."

"Did Marty and his mother get along?"

"Sure they did. No problems that I know of."

"How old is Marty?"

"I guess he's in his thirties. Do you think Marty had something to do with Maggie's disappearance?"

"I don't know, just checking possibilities."

"Okay, but Marty would never do anything to hurt his mother."

"Well, Mrs. Holcombe, that's all I need to ask for now."

"Please call me Ellen. Mrs. Holcombe was my deceased mother-in-law."

"Okay, Ellen."

He rose from the sofa and hurried out the front door into the darkness. It was getting late and I had lost track of the passage of time.

I was glad that Barry and his cohorts were participating in the hunt for Maggie. The more help, the faster the search, but I was going to keep searching no matter what. I was absolutely and positively sure that's what Maggie would want me to do.

"Officer?" I shouted down the dark sidewalk that led to the parked police vehicle.

"Yes, Mrs. Holcombe, I mean, Ellen. Can I help you?" he shouted in return.

"Thanks for the help."

"Sure thing, Ellen. I'll see you soon."

"Yeah, okay. Officer?"

"Yes ma'am."

"Would you like to have a bite to eat? I've made enough for both of us, if you're hungry?" I asked as I tried to be discreet while yelling the invitation down towards the car. "It's fried chicken. Do you like fried chicken?"

"Yes ma'am, I surely do, but I can't stay. I have to go fill out all the paperwork and get the ball rolling on the search."

"Won't the others do that?"

"I'm not sure if they will or not. I just want to make sure all the T's are crossed and the I's are dotted, if you know what I mean? How about a rain check?"

"That would be great. Call me and let me know when it will be convenient for you."

"See you soon, Ellen," he said as he climbed into the police vehicle and waved as he drove off down the road toward the courthouse.

"Why did I do that?" I asked myself as I felt the red from embarrassment travel from my toes to my nose. "There's no fool like an old fool."

I walked into my house where I was greeted by my housemate Nikki.

"Nikki, did you see me acting like a silly school girl? Whatever got into me?"

I held Nikki in my arms and hugged her close to me. She was my friend no matter what. She was my only close friend now that I could not find Maggie.

My mind was so tired of spinning on the carousel of thoughts. Maggie – Barry – the little white house across the street – Barry – Maggie and so on and so on until I was dizzy from trying to keep up with the constant agitation.

"Nikki, let's get ready for bed," I said as I placed her gently on the carpeted floor.

Sleep wasn't going to come easily because my mind refused to stop replaying each and every event of the day.

I heard something that woke me from my restless sleep. I could feel the vibrations of my dog's body as it growled a warning so low that I felt the sound more than I actually heard it.

"What is it, Nikki?" I whispered softly.

Nikki's growl rose in volume slightly but she did not move from her position of being curled up next to me on the bed.

"Are you dreaming, girl?" I asked as I reached to stroke her.

The growling didn't stop as she perked up her ears and tried to absorb all of the sounds inside and outside the house.

I forced myself from the covers and wrapped my body in the robe that I had laid across the foot of my bed and shoed my feet with my slippers. I refused to turn on a light to let anyone know that I was moving about so they would be able to track my movements.

"I don't hear anything, Nikki. Where is it coming from? What is it that you hear?"

Suddenly Nikki erupted into loud barks and went running back and forth through the house as if she were going to chew up everyone and anyone within biting distance.

I heard loud running footfalls leaving my front porch and racing down the sidewalk toward the street.

When I reached the living room, I peeked out the window to see a dark form disappearing from the circle of light beneath the street light that was positioned in front of Maggie's house. I could not determine whether the dark form was a man or a woman. My heart told me it was a man because of the way he held his body that appeared muscular while he was running.

I knew I had to look at my front porch to see if there was anything on it that didn't belong to me. There could be a bomb sitting there, for all I knew, with a timer ticking away the last moments of my life.

"Nikki, why would anyone want to bother me? I haven't done anything wrong. All I want to do is find Maggie," I whimpered as I slowly unlocked and pulled open my front door.

As I looked out my door, the little house across the street caught my eye. I stared intently at what I thought was a light moving around inside the house, a flashlight perhaps, then it was gone. It must have been a reflection off of the street light I reasoned trying to convince myself that I really didn't see anything in the little white house.

I reached for the light switch to illuminate my front porch but thought better of it. Instead, I closed the door quickly, locking it, and walked into the kitchen to retrieve my own flashlight for the purposes of inspecting my front porch.

With flashlight in hand, I decided to exit my house through the back door and walk around to the front. I had myself thoroughly convinced that my front porch would blow my house to smithereens if I set one foot onto it from my living room.

67

It was two o'clock in the morning and I was prowling around outside my house like a would-be robber because I was too afraid to step onto my front porch. The grass was wet with dew and slippery beneath my slippers. I guided myself along the wall of the house with my right hand as I extended my free hand to gain some support. Nikki was trailing behind trying to avoid the moisture hanging heavy on the grass and yet look vigilant, alert, and most of all, protective. She was a funny sight to behold as she stepped gingerly, trying to keep a fierce look on her tiny face.

I peeked around the corner of the house and I smelled something strange. The streetlight glistened off of a huge dark spot or several dark spots looking as if something liquid had been thrown at my front porch.

After a few seconds of searching my mind, I realized that the smell was that of fresh blood.

CHAPTER 6: THE SHADOW GRABBED ME

Nikki growled and suddenly sprang out at a shadow. I screamed like I was going to die at that very moment. The shadow grabbed me by placing both of my upper arms within his firm grip of each hand and gently shook me to get me to open my eyes.

"Ellen, please Ellen, it's me, Marty."

By the time I closed my mouth, I realized it was Marty but I was still scared.

"Marty, what are you doing here?"

"Looking for mom. The cops called me and said she was missing. Do you know anything about this?" he asked as if he were also scared, not just worried.

"I'm the one who called the sheriff. I found Maggie's back door standing open and the back light shining brightly during the daylight hours so I sort of guessed there was something not quite right."

"Is that all?"

"No, I went inside the house and found a note she had written to me telling me to call the police if she didn't get home by a certain time."

"What note? Let me see it. Who was it from?"

"Your mother hid the note in a place where she knew I would look. I can't show it to you because the police have it and it was in your mother's handwriting so it was written by her very own hand."

"Where did she go?"

"The note said she was going to a flea market that was set up around the skating rink to meet someone. It was someone you had a problem with when you were a teenager. She said she thought everything had been settled. You wouldn't know who that might be, would you?"

"No, I don't remember anyone that would call now. I did get into trouble once but that's long over with."

"I'm worried about her. I thought maybe you might know something, anything at all, that might help."

"No, nothing. I have no idea why she's not here. She didn't call me back after I left her a message. When I got the call from the cops, I was worried, too."

"Why don't you come into my house. I've got to call the police. Someone threw blood on my front porch. It wasn't you, was it?" I asked as I tried to see the expression on his face.

"No, not me. I wouldn't do anything like that to you," he answered me angrily.

"I didn't think you would, Marty, but I had to ask."

"Yeah, sure."

"Come on in. The police have your mom's house yellow taped and no one is supposed to go inside. You came walking from around back. Did you go inside her house for anything?"

"No, no, I was just looking around, that's all. I didn't go inside," he answered me as he looked toward the ground.

I started to walk to the back of my house toward the back door, "Come on, Marty, follow me. I don't want to track through the blood."

"No thanks, Ellen. I've got to go home and get some sleep. I've got to work tomorrow."

"You're not going to help look for your mother?"

"What can I do that the police aren't doing?"

"Well, you've got a point there. I'm supposed to work tomorrow but I'm going to do some searching of my own."

"Do you think you should?"

"Yes, I do. I'm sure your mother would expect her best friend not to give up. But, you go on to work. I'll call you if I find out anything. Your number is in the book, isn't it?"

"Yes, it is. How do you think the police called me?"

"Well, like I said, I'll call if I find out anything. Right now I'm calling the police. If you don't want to be here, you'd better leave now."

"Bye, Ellen. Call me, okay?"

"Sure, go on now."

I watched Marty walk to the street. He must have parked his car several doors down because I didn't see it anywhere.

"Nikki girl, Marty was acting sort of strange. I wonder why? He didn't seem to be very worried about his mother's disappearance. Why in the world was he skulking around his mother's house at two in the morning? His explanation sounded like a lie."

I returned to the interior of my house where I illuminated all of the corners of it with every overhead light or table lamp available.

"This is Ellen Holcombe, I need to report that someone threw blood on my front porch."

"Your address?"

"305 Valleyview Street."

"Someone will be there to talk to you shortly."

"Is Officer Barry Johnson on duty?"

"Yes ma'am."

"Do you think he could come by the house?"

"I'll check to see if he is available. If he can't go to 305 Valleyview, I'll send the closest vehicle."

"Thank you."

I sat in my easy chair in the living room, holding Nikki on my lap, and waited. I was near to dozing off to sleep when I heard my name being shouted.

"Mrs. Holcombe."

I was startled at first, because I expected my doorbell to ring.

"Mrs. Holcombe, Ellen Holcombe."

I ran to the door and peered out the small window where I saw Barry standing on my sidewalk. I quickly turned the lock and yanked on the doorknob.

"Stay in there, Ellen. I don't want you tracking through that mess. We need to find out what it is, for sure."

"Okay, Barry. I'll go around to the back."

I glanced down at my robe and slippers and decided it was time I slipped into something else. I didn't need to be parading around outside in front of Barry in my shabby old robe and worn slippers.

I went to my bedroom and pulled on some jeans and a pullover top. Then I ran to the bathroom where I rubbed sleep from my face with cold water and pulled a comb through my wild looking hair. Finally, I was ready to go outside and talk to Barry.

I walked around the house toward the front carrying Nikki in my arms.

When Barry saw me he asked, "When did this happen?"

"Somewhere between one and two this morning. Nikki woke me up with her growling."

"Did you see anybody?"

"By the time I got in here to look out the front window, I saw a body clad in black under that street light over there."

"You didn't get a good look?"

"No, he was too far away."

"You said "he". How could you tell it was a man?"

"Only by the way he was moving around. It didn't look like the movements of a woman. I couldn't see his face at all."

"Could you tell how tall he was?"

"I could guess maybe six feet."

"Hair?"

"Covered with something black, a stocking cap or hood."

"Hands? Were they white or dark skinned?"

"Covered with black gloves."

"Boy, you're no help at all," he said with a smile.

"I know."

"Do you know why anyone would do this?"

"No, no idea."

"Have you made someone mad at you recently?"

"Not that I know of except maybe that person who called me?"

"Who was that?"

"I don't really know. When you get finished out here, come inside and I'll tell you everything I know."

I could see the dark night sky starting to streak with the rays of daylight.

Barry went to the police vehicle and extracted a camera. He took some photographs of the mess and then proceeded to take some samples of the blood for testing.

"Where's your garden hose, Ellen?"

"On the side of the house, I'll get it for you."

He sprayed the cold water onto the blood spots washing them away and forcing the bloody watery liquid down the driveway to the drain along the street. With that job completed, I asked him to come inside so I could tell him about the little white house across the street.

"I don't know how much you know about me, Barry, but what I'm going to tell you doesn't make sense to me at all. I'm a writer in my spare time and I have a very vivid imagination all the time, but I haven't been able to figure out the secret of the little white house across the street at all. It's not because I haven't tried, because I have. The threatening phone calls are the result of my searching through records and generally snooping around to find the truth."

"Are you talking about the house that sits empty most of the time just across the street from you?"

"Yep, that's the one."

"Nobody lives there. How can that be a problem? It's just an empty house and a well-kept empty house. Who keeps it up?"

"That's one of the questions I wanted answered."

"Start at the beginning, Ellen. You've managed to get my interest big time."

"Like I said, I'm a writer and as a writer I tend to turn over rocks, a lot of rocks, until I can find what I'm looking for. It all started when I watched, on a couple of different occasions, the movement of furniture back and forth from the little white house across the street. I saw the moving men, it looked like four youngish men, and there might have been a woman in the group, clad in matching uniforms with the moving company name emblazoned on the back and the worker's name written above the left pocket. It was Diamond Movers and they are not listed in the phone book. Of course, they could have been from out of town and, in that case, I wouldn't have found a listing. I checked the Internet – nothing. Then I saw a police car parked out front of the house and I was happy to think that a police officer might be moving in there. No such luck, the police officer, I assume it was a police officer and not the chief of police himself, left and then I received a strange phone call."

"Did you see the officer good enough to be able to describe him to me?"

"No, I only saw him from the back. I believe it was a him because the hips were not rounded like a woman's would be."

"All right, what was the phone call?"

"The phone call was strange because all the person wanted to know was if I was the resident at 305 Valleyview Street? I answered yes without a thought. I know I shouldn't have done that but the question caught me off guard. Sounds silly, doesn't it?"

"Don't ever answer that kind of question again," said Barry sternly.

"I won't but that was only the beginning. That same night I went to bed and was awakened when Nikki started growling and getting really upset at someone or something. That was at four o'clock in the morning."

"Did you see anyone?"

"No, but I trust Nikki's ears. She heard someone, and that someone was prowling around my house at four in the morning."

"You didn't call the cops, did you?"

"No, what was I going to tell you guys? You would only think I was a lonely old widow looking for a little extra attention, now wouldn't you?"

"No, I wouldn't."

"Maybe not you, but the others would."

"You should have called anyway?"

"Well, I'm not going to worry about that. I've got other things on my mind."

"You should worry about that, Ellen."

"Okay, okay, I will but I'll do it later. To go on with my story – I told my friend at work about the prowler and she suggested that he might have bugged my phone. I first thought she was crazy but the more I thought about it, I wasn't so sure. I know a lot of stuff nowadays is done electronically but maybe he wasn't so technologically advanced. An old-fashioned wiretap that led to some kind of recorder was what I was thinking of. Or, maybe, he even planted a bomb. You've got to remember that I'm a writer and I do make dramatic enormous jumps to unusual conclusions."

"A bomb? You're not serious?"

"Well, I didn't know what he did if he did anything."

"What's next?"

"I looked at the connection box for the telephone outside my house but I didn't know what I was looking at. That wasn't any help at all. It only made me more anxious.

"Then I got interested in the little white house across the street. I started snooping around there to see if I could find out if anybody was living there. I have seen movers carrying furnishings into the house and the police person but I hadn't seen the inhabitants."

"What got you onto that topic?"

"Curiosity mostly. Just being nosy, I guess. Things just didn't seem right around that place, if you know what I mean? So – I started checking by going to the courthouse and looking up the deed."

"You didn't?"

"Yes, I did. I used to work for a lawyer so I knew how to do it."

"Most people don't know they can do that."

"Then – I received another phone call that told me not be watching the house or checking the courthouse records. The voice said it was a warning."

"You didn't call the police then, either, did you?"

"And say what? That a mysterious voice warned me not to snoop anymore?"

"You're right. There hasn't been any direct threat, has there. The underlying danger seems obvious."

"Then Maggie disappeared."

"Do you think they're related?"

"I don't have any idea. I don't see how they could be."

"You said you were a writer? Did you add anything to this or embellish it in any way to make it more mysterious?"

"Barry, if I did anything, I left a few things out."

"I'm not a believer in coincidence, Ellen. Too much is happening to not be related, don't you think?"

I shook my head in agreement.

Barry left to return to the police station and I was alone again except for Nikki.

CHAPTER 7: RIGHT NICE FELLA

I looked at the clock after I saw Barry's car pull away from the curb. It was almost time to get ready for work. I had worked many times without much sleep, I guess I could do it again. I was way too wound up to even think about closing my eyes and turning off the workings of my overwhelmed brain.

Nikki was so nervous. She was at my side every minute during the night time activities and she stayed under my feet while I was trying to dress for work.

"What's the matter, Nikki?" I asked my sidekick as she looked at me with beseeching eyes telling me that she didn't want to be left alone in that big, old, lonely house. My heart melted because I knew she was scared. "Don't worry, girl. I'm taking you with me. If they want to fire me, they can. I will not leave you here. Someone is liable to hurt you and I certainly can't have that."

I poked Nikki down into a tote bag I carried occasionally to work and walked into the office with my head held high.

The workday was long and tedious but I managed to get through it with the help of my friend, Sylvia.

"Ellen, what was going on at your house last night?" asked Sylvia trying very hard to control her curiosity.

"How did you know anything happened?"

"Mary in Finance called me before I left the house. She thought you might not come in to work today."

"How did she know anything happened?"

"Her husband has a police scanner."

"What did they tell you happened?"

"Not much because they didn't want to broadcast it. They just said something about blood at your house."

"Yeah, blood, that's what it was."

"Whose blood?"

I don't have any idea. It might not even be a who. It could be a what. They weren't sure if it was animal or human. They were going to test it today."

"Well, are you going to tell me what happened?"

"I'll tell you what I can and that really isn't very much as far as the blood is concerned."

"Go on, tell me already,"

"Someone threw blood onto my front porch. That's all that happened."

"You're kidding? Why would someone do that?"

"I don't know. But, I believe that I have made a big time enemy somewhere along the line."

"Who?"

"You got me. If I could answer that question maybe I could put a stop to this silliness."

"Has anything else happened?"

"Just a couple of phone calls and the prowler. Remember? I told you about the prowler."

"What are you going to do?"

"Bring my dog with me when I come to work every day. I'm afraid to leave her at home. Someone might want to do her some harm. That's about all I can do except call the cops which is what I've already done."

"What did they say?"

"They'll investigate. But, who knows? They may not ever find out who did it or why?"

"Where are you going to stay?"

"At home, where else?"

"Aren't you afraid?"

"Scared to death."

"Why don't you stay with your son?"

"And pull him into this mess? No way."

"I don't think I would stay at your house, not after the blood."

"I don't have a choice," I answered and quickly changed the subject. "Have you ever met a Town Police Officer named Barry Johnson?"

"I've not actually met him, but I know who he is."

"What do you know about him?"

"Why?"

"He seems like a right nice fella, if you know what I mean."

"You met him?" asked Sylvia with a mischievous smile.

"Yeah, he's the one who has been helping me with this mess."

"He is a right nice fella. He's a widower, you know. His wife died of cancer a couple of years back. She's been dead long enough so that his dating someone new wouldn't be a problem in the eyes of the narrow minded boobs in this small town."

"He is footloose and fancy free. I'm glad to hear that."

"You're really interested in him, aren't you?"

"Well, he has been a big help to me. He seems to be paying me a little more attention than he would have if he were married or I still was."

"He'd be a good catch if that's what you're looking for."

"I'm not sure what I'm looking for. I've got my sidekick, Nikki. I don't necessarily need the companionship of a man," I said with a smile of deceit.

"Yeah, sure," added Sylvia.

Four-thirty finally made an appearance on my clock and I grabbed my handbag and dog and headed for home with the thoughts of going to sleep. I was so tired from being awake most of the night and working the entire day.

When I pulled into my driveway I saw the gray, ordinary sedan parked in front of the little white house across the street. I could see two figures sitting inside the car watching me. Then I remembered.

"Oh God, I forgot about the FBI," I mumbled to Nikki as I scrambled to climb from my vehicle.

I walked to my front door and fumbled with my key as I tried to watch the two figures exit their ordinary gray car that was parked across the street in front of the little white house which was actually the back of the little white house.

I pushed the door open and nearly tripped over a lamp that was lying on the floor directly in my path.

"Oh, Nikki, look at this mess."

I was crying now. How much more of this abuse could I handle?

While I was standing and staring, the two figures walked up my sidewalk and stood behind me taking in the same view of destruction that I was seeing.

"What happened here?" asked one of the figures.

"I just got here. You saw me drive up. How am I supposed to know?" I answered sarcastically. "Who are you?" I said as I whirled around to face them.

"I'm Agent Thompson, this is Agent Chandler. We're with the FBI," he said as he flashed a wallet containing a badge and some identification in front of my eyes.

"Let me see that," I said as I reached for the identification wallet he was moving away from me toward his pocket.

He handed the identification back to me so that I could get a better look.

"Too many strange things have been happening to me. I want to make sure you are who you say you are," I said as I tried to read the small print that told where his office was headquartered. "Do you work out of Richmond?"

"I see you've done some checking."

"Yes sir, I have. Where on here does it tell me where you work?"

"Right here," he said as he pointed to a corner.

"Okay, now that your identity has been established, why do you want to talk to me?"

"Who did this to your house?"

"I don't know but I should be calling the Town Police right now."

"Hold off on that for a moment, Mrs. Holcombe. We have just a couple of questions that we need to get out of the way before anyone else gets involved."

I was beginning to lose my patience. Nikki was hovering next to me shaking as if she were trying to rattle her joints enough to disconnect them forcing her to become a pile of disjointed bones.

I forced the two men outside to my front porch and closed my door behind me. If they weren't going to help me, I didn't want them seeing anything else inside my house. Stubbornness had reared its ugly head again.

"I would ask you inside to have a seat but you've seen the problem. What questions?"

"Mrs. Holcombe, do you know who lives in the little white house across the street?"

"No, I don't."

"Have you seen the people who live there?"

"I saw the movers and I saw a woman with dark hair."

"Would you be able to identify any of those people?"

"No, it was too dark. I wasn't able to see any facial features."

"You haven't seen any other activity?"

"No, why are you asking?"

"We are unable to divulge that information, Mrs. Holcombe."

"Well, I'm not able to divulge anything else. So, if you two will excuse me, I've got to call the police," I said angrily as I turned to reenter my house.

"Mrs. Holcombe, one more moment, please."

"Okay, okay, what now?"

"I'll leave my card with you. If you see anyone go in or out of that house, please call me no matter what time of day or night."

"Sure, sure, okay, now please let me call the police and get some help."

I looked at the card as the two men walked away from me towards their car. Something wasn't kosher about this whole thing. I knew this was something else I was going to have to tell Barry.

I smiled when I thought about Barry.

Nikki and I watched the two men drive away before I entered my house to try and locate my telephone.

When I called my house a mess, I wasn't exaggerating. The lamps were knocked over onto the floor, anything breakable such as the glass figurines and vases were shattered, the cushions were pulled from the sofa but, thankfully, they had not been slashed with the long butcher knife I spotted near the doorway to the kitchen. I couldn't find anything resembling a telephone in the living room so I proceeded to the dining room.

The dishes that had been displayed in the hutch were all broken. My mother's china was no longer a proud possession that I could pass on to my boys. Even the glass fronts of the hutch had been broken. I guess they were trying to search beneath and behind the dishes as fast as possible. That meant taking your arm and sweeping the contents of each shelf to the floor. But why? What did they want? Or did they want anything at all? Maybe they were just being mean.

Again, I could find no telephone so I reluctantly entered the kitchen. All boxed or bagged items had been opened and scattered helter-skelter across the kitchen floor. Noodles, rice, cereal, flour, sugar, coffee, and anything dry that could be added to the mix was piled on top.

Angry tears were rolling down my cheeks as I searched for the wall mounted telephone and a chair so I could sit before I fell to the floor.

"Operator, this is an emergency. Please get the police for me," I said as I dropped the receiver to the floor and exploded with sobs that would have frightened anyone who might have been passing by the house.

A few moments later I heard sirens and realized that the operator must have been able to determine who placed the call and sent the police to help me.

"Mrs. Holcombe, Ellen Holcombe, this is the police," shouted Officer Barry Johnson as he stood outside my front door with gun drawn and ready to shoot.

"Barry, Barry," I sobbed, "please come on in. There's no one in here except me." The tears would not stop. I struggled to get my breath and try to explain what I didn't know nor understand to Officer Barry Johnson.

"Ellen? Are you all right? You aren't hurt are you?" he asked as he holstered his weapon and slowly entered the living room. "My God! What happened?"

"I don't know," I cried.

"Did you just get here?"

"Yeah, a few minutes ago. It was like this when I walked in. What am I going to do? Why is someone doing this to me?"

"I'm going out to the car to get a camera. It's in the trunk. I want to take some pictures of this mess for you for your insurance company. Does the whole house look like this?"

"I haven't checked the bedrooms yet. I'm afraid to see what they did in there to all of my personal things."

"You just stay there. Sit on that chair and hold your scared little dog. I'm going to take a look in there for you," he said as a walked down the hallway. He reached for his gun again, drew it from the holster, and foisted it out in front of him before he pushed the door of the first bedroom with his foot.

When he entered the room he swung the weapon from side to side grasping it with both hands ready and willing to shoot the intruder without much provocation. When he found no one in the room he proceeded further down the hall to the next bedroom. He performed the same routine again until he was satisfied that no one was lurking under the beds or hiding in the closets of each of the three bedrooms.

"Ellen, the rooms are in bad shape. All the drawers have been turned over to the floor, closets have been emptied, and bedding has been strewn everywhere. You're going to need some help getting this place back into living condition."

"I don't want any help. I'm afraid if anyone came to my aid, she or he might get hurt. I'll have to do it myself," I answered as I was trying to fight another wave of gut wrenching sobs.

"When I get off work this evening at midnight, I'll go home and get a few hours of sleep. Then I'll come help you for three or four hours before I go back to work. Maybe I could help you get this cleaned up so it's livable again."

"I couldn't ask you to do that, you're a police officer."

"Yes, I'm a police officer, but I'm also a friend, I hope."

I tried to smile to let him know how much I appreciated those words, but the tears were too forceful and too plentiful.

"Do you have someone you could spend the night with tonight?"

"My son, but I definitely don't want to put him into any danger."

"I don't think that will be a problem. Whoever is harassing you, wants to take care of the problem right here in this house from the looks of it. No one has bothered you at work, have they?"

"No, come to think of it, I've not had any problems at work."

"That's what I mean. I'm sure whoever is causing you the problems knows where you work. That would be easy enough to find out, you know. All they would have to do is follow you."

"Okay, I'll go stay with my son tonight, just tonight. But, keep it in mind that I'm not going to let somebody scare me from living in my own house," I said fiercely as the stubbornness made itself visible in full force.

Barry wrote down the information he needed for filing a report of a break in and destruction of my property.

Then he had to return to the police station for the remainder of the evening to cover for the dispatcher who had to leave early.

I grabbed an overnight bag, locked up my house, and started driving toward my son's house. Before I had driven very far, I made a quick turn, and headed in the opposite direction. I didn't want him involved in my mess. I decided to stay at a motel that was located in the same town where my house was located. I wanted to stay close and I was sure the owners would give me a good rate to stay there a couple of days so I could get the mess cleaned up in my house.

Ruby's Motel- that was the name of the place. I had heard many, many rumors about the activities that occurred at or around the motel, but I had no real proof that it wasn't just something someone made up from watching too much television. Now, I was going to find out for myself, not because I wanted to for any kind of research I was doing.

When I entered the office to register for a room, I received a strange suspicious look from the clerk because I was a local. My address and driver's license indicated that I lived two blocks away from the motel.

"How long will you be staying, ma'am?" asked the near teenager as he gave me the once over from head to toe.

"I'm not sure. I'm having some work done on my house. I can't stay there until it is complete. I'm allergic. What room is it?"

"212, second on the end. It's a little quieter back there than closer to the office."

"I'd rather have a room closer to the front. Do you have any?"

"Sure, if you'd rather hear the traffic."

"It's the light I'm after, I want to park my car under the light and I want the door and path to my room illuminated as well."

"Okay, no problem. You'll get all the light where this room is located. 201 is directly above this office."

"That's great, thanks," I said as I grabbed the key and walked out the door.

What I was going to do about my problem or problems, I had no idea. All I knew was that Nikki and I were going to get a good night's sleep, I hoped, in a motel not too far away from our home. When we arose from bed the next morning, we were going out to face the world head on with no questions asked about survival. We were going to survive no matter what. We were also going to make sure that Maggie wasn't forgotten. I was going to continue my search for my best friend. I was going to find an answer.

I sneaked Nikki into my motel room from the car. I carried her down inside the tote bag so no one passing me would be able to determine that I was carrying contraband.

"Don't make any barking noises, Nikki. They don't allow dogs to stay here so you've got to be quiet," I said as I lovingly stroked my tired little dog.

I called the town police station and left my phone number for Barry so he would be able to call me if he needed me for any reason whether it was about my break in or about Maggie.

I called my son and left a message on his answering machine so he would know where to find me.

Then, Nikki and I got ready for bed.

The nighttime noises at the motel were plentiful but that didn't matter to either of us.

CHAPTER 8: NIKKI AND I, A MATCHED SET

I made a telephone call to the school board office the next morning to let them know that I was taking a vacation day. What vacation? I really didn't want to spend my valuable down time cleaning up that mess that was made inside my home.

My home wasn't really special other than the fact that it was mine, well, almost mine.

My husband and I were the recipients of the first Habitat for Humanity built house in Stillwell County. Was I ashamed that that was the only way I was ever going to be able to be a homeowner? No way. I was proud. I was so proud that I wanted to erect a blinking neon sign shouting out the reality that "Ellen Holcombe is the proud owner of the first Habitat House built in Stillwell County". I didn't build a sign, I don't think my neighbors would have appreciated the thought behind it. But shame wasn't the reason it was never done.

"Come on, Nikki girl. We're going home to start cleaning up the mess," I told my little excited dog as she pranced and danced around my feet.

I locked the door to my rented motel room behind me as my dog and I walked to the car. It did both of us good to be away from the fear and the fright of my house for one evening. I wanted to put the relief of not being at home to a stop, because I wanted to be able to go home and feel as though I'm not going to be attacked or possibly killed.

If things went well while we were cleaning up, maybe Nikki and I would check out of the motel later in the day and stay home - then again, maybe not.

When I pulled into the driveway, I saw a strange car sitting about two doors down from my lot.

"Looks like someone is sitting in that car," I said to Nikki as I tried to glance at the car without being too obvious.

Nikki's ears perked straight up and she started smelling the air.

I had to laugh at the way she was trying to take care of me by checking out the sights, sounds, and smells in the air.

When I climbed from my car, my watcher made no move.

"Maybe he's a policeman," I said softly to Nikki as I carried her toward my front door.

I inserted the key into the lock and used that moment to glance behind to see if my watcher was following my path up the sidewalk.

"Must be a cop."

I entered my distressed home, kicking broken pieces of glassware and ceramic out of my path, as I walked to my front windows where I pulled the blinds up to their highest point fastening them into position. I unlocked and tugged at each window until I had all of the openings into my house open allowing the curtains and draperies to flap in the breeze.

I continued to monitor the vehicle because the passenger remained inside and appeared to be watching my every move.

"Nikki, hopefully Barry will be here soon and we will be able to determine if the watcher is another cop. I'll find a piece of paper and write down the license number on the vehicle, just for safety reasons. Better to be safe than sorry, I say. How about you, girl?"

I located my trash bags and started loading up the broken pieces of everything. I had to be careful because the sharp edges of the glass and ceramic would slice right through the thin plastic sheeting and I would continue to add to the mess rather than make it disappear.

I had been working for over an hour when I decided to check on the watcher.

He was still there looking as though he had never moved, not one little bit.

"Nikki, I wonder if the watcher is all right. I never see the guy move."

I returned to my loading of trash bags when I heard a vehicle pull into my driveway.

"I bet that is Barry," I said to my dog as an enormous smile appeared on my face.

I walked to the front door where I saw my eldest son standing waiting for me to appear.

"Mom, what happened?" he asked as he entered my living room.

"Someone must have got mad at me about something," I responded with a laugh.

"Who did this?"

"I don't know, Eddy. I came home from work yesterday and it was like this. As a matter of fact, I've cleaned a lot of it up at this point. You should have seen it yesterday?"

"Where did you stay last night? I didn't recognize the telephone number that you left on my answering machine."

"I spent the night at the motel a couple of blocks over from here. I wanted to stay close in case something else happened."

"Do you think anything else will happen?" he demanded.

"Eddy, I didn't think this would happen. I don't remember pissing anybody off, not lately anyway," I answered with a weak laugh.

"You don't have any idea why this is happening? Nothing? Nada?"

"No, unless it's related to Maggie's disappearance. I told you Maggie is missing, didn't I?" I asked knowing what his answer would be.

"No, Mom, you didn't tell me anything about Maggie being missing. When did this happen?"

"A couple of days ago, after I started checking on that little white house across the street."

"Why were you checking on that house?" he asked as he glanced out my living room window to get an image of the house I was talking about.

"Something's strange about that place, even the FBI think so."

"The FBI? When did you talk to the FBI?" he asked excitedly.

"Yesterday, right after I got home and found this mess."

"Are they investigating the break in? Why would the FBI investigate a break in, mom?"

"No, they aren't investigating the break in. They were asking me questions about that house," I said loudly as I pointed toward the little white house across the street that was looming large like a specter of evil in my mind.

"Did Maggie's disappearance have anything to do with that house?" he snapped.

"I don't know."

"Is anybody looking into what happened here?" he asked softly as he tried to control the tone of his voice.

"Yes, I called the town police. They are doing the best they can, Eddy. I think that's a cop sitting across the street over there," I whispered as I gestured toward the window.

Eddy leaned to the window and looked, wide-eyed, at the great outdoors.

"What cop? I don't see a cop."

"Did you see a car parked over there when you got here?"

"No, I don't remember one."

"Well, there was one parked there for at least a couple of hours. He kept watching me, my house, I mean."

"Are you sure it was a cop?"

"No," I answered apprehensively. "Maybe it wasn't. I'll ask Barry when he gets here."

"Barry? Who is Barry?"

"A friend."

"What kind of friend?"

"A cop friend. Nothing else, just a friend," Ellen answered with a smile.

"Are you finally going to see someone, mom?"

"He hasn't asked me yet."

"If he does, are you going?"

"I think so. I'll make up my mind if and when the time comes."

"You want me to stay and help you?"

"No, why are you here anyway?"

"Well, I called you at work and they said you had taken a vacation day. I drove by earlier but your car wasn't here. I ran a couple of errands and decided to stop by again. This time you were here with all of this mess."

"Did you need something?"

"Yeah, I needed to know where you were calling from last night. Like I said, I didn't recognize the phone number."

"Okay, there is nothing wrong is there?" I asked trying to make sure he didn't have a problem that he wasn't telling me.

"No, mom. I'm not the one with the problem or should I say problems. Why don't you come stay with me a couple of days. I'll sleep on the couch and you can have the bed."

"No, honey, please. I don't want you involved in this mess. Especially since I don't know what this mess is."

"Why would I be involved? You would be spending the night. That's all."

"Well, what if they found me at your house? Would they do this to you? I don't want this to happen to you. I'll stay at the motel again tonight then I am coming right back here tomorrow."

"You can't stay here by yourself."

"I won't. Nikki will be here with me."

"You're joking."

"No, I'm not joking. I can't let some fool chase me away from my home. I worked too hard to get this home and I plan to keep it, no matter what. I'm also going to find Maggie and I'm going to find out what's going on at that little white house across the street," I said as I squared my jaw and exhibited the stubborn determination that Eddy knew I had in spades.

"Mom, what if something happens again?"

"I'll call the police."

"You need to get a cell phone, mom. You need to get a small one so you can put it in your pocket at all times. You probably need to get one of those emergency call buttons to wear around your neck. You know, the kind of thing that the old people get when they live alone and are too old to get up when they fall. You've seen them on those television commercials. You know what I'm talking about, don't you?"

"Yeah, but I won't get one. I'm not that old, Eddy. I still work and I'm not feeble of body or mind," I answered angrily.

"I'm not saying you are. What if someone hits you over the head? You might need help."

"No, I won't get one and that's that. Now, you go on to work. I'll be fine. I don't want you hanging around here so that whoever is doing this will get any ideas about going after you. Do you understand me?"

"Okay, okay, but call me every hour, mom. If you don't call, I'll either come by or send the cops. Do you understand me?"

I shook my head in agreement as I tried to hide the tears of pride my son had caused to appear in my eyes. I was so very glad he loved me.

"I love you," I said as I hugged him as tight as I could. "Now, you go on to work."

He turned and left me standing at my front door.

I was so relieved to see him walking down that sidewalk. I would die, absolutely die, if anything happened to him because of something I did, or maybe, didn't do.

I went back to cleaning up the mess.

I heard another vehicle pull into my driveway. Nikki started barking her fool head off and I took that as a sign whoever it was brought new smells wafting in to Nikki's nose. I was hoping that Barry would be the one arriving, but I didn't think Nikki would get so bent out of shape if he were coming. She had been around him several times and knew what smells he brought with him.

I walked to the front door and looked out to see a stranger, a man, sitting in his parked car in my driveway. The car looked like the same one that had been parked on the street with the passenger watching me.

"Good girl," I said to Nikki as I looked around for something to use as a weapon. Then I remembered the baseball bat. "Let's get our booger-banger."

I had latched the front storm door from the inside so I knew I would be able to tell if anyone was coming inside the house while I was trying to locate the bat. When I returned with bat in hand to the living room, I spotted the man walking around to the side of the house to the back door.

102

I hadn't latched that one.

I ran as fast as I could and snapped the lock before he arrived and reached for the door handle. When I looked up from the locking mechanism, he was standing directly in front of me on the other side of the glass.

He looked disheveled, over wrought, as if he had the whole wide world sitting on his sagging shoulders. He appeared to be dressed in a navy blue work uniform that was covered on the upper part of his body by a worn, dirty jacket. The uniform looked like the one the four movers had been wearing. There had to be thousands of sets of those blue uniform work clothes in the area.

A moment of pity passed through my mind but it was quickly pushed aside by fear.

I screamed and grabbed for the big heavy wooden door.

"Are you Ellen Holcombe?" asked the stranger.

I slowed the progress of the closing door and said, "Who are you?"

"I'm Maggie's ex-husband. I'm Jeremy Boothe."

I didn't close the door.

"Why are you here?"

"I'm trying to find Maggie? Have you seen her?"

"What do you want?"

"Maggie, I want Maggie."

"She's missing. I've called the police and they are trying to find her."

The stranger was ready to collapse. I could see the pain and anguish as it filled his mind and heart and coated his eyes with sadness.

"I'm too late. He said he was going to find her. I didn't have anything to do with it. I swear I didn't. She must have recognized him from the newspaper article I left for her to see." he said as he staggered and fell to the floor of my back porch.

"Ellen! Ellen! Are you here?" I heard from the direction of my front porch.

"Wait right there, Mr. Boothe, I'm going to the front to let in the police so you can talk to them."

"No, no, I can't talk to the police," he yelled at my back.

I ran to the front door and snapped the latch to allow Barry to enter the house.

"Come with me, Barry. There is a man at the back door who says he is Maggie's ex-husband."

"You shouldn't be letting any strangers in the house," he scolded.

"I didn't. That's why he is at the back door."

When we arrived at the back door, the man was gone. Barry asked me to step aside and he exited the back door looking for the stranger. He was nowhere in sight.

Barry came back into the house, latched the door again, and walked to the front just in time to see the man driving his car across my front yard in his effort to get off my driveway because Barry's car had him blocked in.

"I didn't get his plates," shouted Barry as he watched the vehicle fade into the distance.

"I did," I said as I held up the little slip on which I had written the combination of numbers and alphabet characters. "I saw the car parked outside my house for several hours. I thought you had sent someone to keep an eye on my house."

Barry looked at the paper and declared, "It's a rental. The car is a rental."

"You can tell that from the plate number?"

"Yes, but I'll call it in and see who rented it."

"I wonder if he is Maggie's ex."

"I thought you told me her husband was dead."

"I did. That's what I thought, but obviously I was assuming the wrong thing."

"Yeah, if this guy is telling you the truth."

"Why wouldn't he be?" I asked as I felt the hackles on the back of my neck start to rise.

"Your friend Maggie lied to you didn't she?"

"About what?" I was getting defensive now.

"About her ex-husband."

"She didn't tell me anything. Nothing. Not one word. I assumed he was dead. I didn't know he was an ex and she never told me there was an ex."

"Well, that's another form of lie, isn't it?"

"What are you talking about, Barry?"

"She omitted the truth."

"Don't be silly. I never asked and she didn't tell. There was no lying involved," I said angrily.

"Calm down, Ellen, just calm down. All I'm trying to do is help."

"I don't think calling Maggie a liar is helping, not one little bit."

"Forget I said anything."

"I'll try. Have you found out anything about her whereabouts?"

"No, me and another officer have been doing a lot of checking, but nothing yet. Officer Stone is going to visit Maggie Boothe's son today. He set up an appointment with him at two o'clock this afternoon. I'll give him a call later to see if anything new has turned up."

"This really doesn't sound very good, does it?"

"No. No one has received any kind of ransom demand. You know it's not about money; at this point any way."

"What could it be? Why did someone take her away from here?"

"Maybe they didn't take her away from here? She's just not at home. Do you know of anyone else with whom she might have a close relationship, like you with her, I mean?"

"No, she always called me her best friend, her only true friend. She knew people, a lot of people, because she was a retired school teacher. But true friends on whom she could depend, she always said that had to be me."

"Well, I'll check in later. In the mean time we'd better get this mess cleaned up. You've done a lot of it already. What time did you get here?"

"Nikki and I couldn't sleep so we got here pretty early."

When Nikki heard her name she whimpered from her perch on the sofa pillow in the only clean corner in the room.

"What would you do without that little dog?" asked Barry as he witnessed the love that pulsed through the air from animal creature to human creature and back again.

"I don't know and I don't even want to think about it," I said softly.

We worked until noon and then decided to break for lunch.

"I'll go pick us something up and bring it right back. Would that be all right with you?"

"Yes, that would be great. What are you getting?"

"What would you like?"

"Two hamburgers, one for me and one for Nikki. She's worked hard, too. You have to know it's hard lying there on the sofa pillow for so many hours watching after the both of us," I said with a laugh.

Before we could change our minds, Barry left for the food and I continued to survey the remaining mess. It was now confined to the bedrooms. The rest of the house was in tolerable condition.

While Barry was in the house with me, I felt safe and secure. Now that he was gone for a few minutes, worry settled over me to such a point that Nikki sensed the change and she, too, became agitated and restless.

I was tired. I pulled a chair up next to the kitchen table, held my little dog in my lap, and cried. I needed those few moments to let go – a release.

I heard the car pull into my driveway and jumped up to wipe the tears from my face.

"Time to eat, Nikki," I said as I walked to the door to let Barry into my house and my heart.

I picked at my hamburger until I finally got it eaten. Then I broke Nikki's burger up into tiny little pieces and fed them to her. Barry laughed at me for treating my little dog so special.

"You just have to learn to live with it, Barry. We are a matched set, you know," I said with a youthful giggle.

"You aren't going to stay here tonight, are you?"

"No, I'm so tired. I think I'll stay at the motel again tonight. If someone tried to break in while I was here asleep, I'm afraid I wouldn't be able to wake up to hear them. I don't think Nikki would be much help either."

"That's good, at least it will give me another night without worrying about someone bothering you again. Hopefully, whoever this pest is doesn't know you're staying at the motel."

"If he wants me bad enough, he will be able to find the car in the parking lot."

"Do you think it might be Maggie's ex that's doing this to you?"

"No, I don't think so. Just a gut feeling, but I don't think he wants anything bad to happen to Maggie or me for that matter. He was really distraught when I told him Maggie was missing. He said something peculiar in response. He said he was too late. I wonder what that means. Oh yeah, he was dressed in the same kind of clothes the movers used. I couldn't see any company name though because of the jacket he wore."

"I hope you're right, but if it isn't him, I can't imagine who it could be."

"Neither can I," I added sadly.

We finally finished the bedrooms and prepared to leave for the night.

"Barry, I'll be at the motel. I'm sure you have the number. It's the first room in the front on the second floor."

"Do you want me to check on you later tonight?"

"You can if you want to."

"I want to," he said as he drew me to his warm body and hugged me. "That surely feels good to hold someone close again."

"Yeah, I know what you mean," I agreed as I returned the hug clinging to him much longer than I should have.

"I'll call you later," he told me as he watched me climb into my car.

I watched him get into his car and back out of the driveway, so I could do the same.

Nikki was so tired she had already fallen asleep on the front seat of the car.

Even though my body was so very tired, my mind was wide awake. I decided to cruise around for a few minutes to see if I could see anything that was different or that looked out of the ordinary. Maybe that would help me find Maggie or find the idiot who was harassing me.

CHAPTER 9: THE BEHEMOTH

My mind was working overtime while my body was screaming for rest. I drove slowly, cautiously peering into the darkest holes, blinking under the brightest of street lights, searching for what? I had no clue. I was just searching. I was hoping to find something, anything that would point me into the right direction. What was the right direction? Again, I didn't have a clue.

Headlights from a vehicle that was higher off the ground than my car were shining brightly into my rearview mirror.

"Back off, idiot," I mumbled.

The headlights were positioned in my rearview mirror. The vehicle remained behind me not slowing down, speeding up, or turning. It remained steadfastly in my rearview mirror.

I slowed down my speed hoping the brightly lit behemoth would pass me as he endeavored to travel on his way to wherever.

"Damn!" I shouted as the behemoth slowed to match my speed.

"Step on it, Ellen," I told myself as I pressed the gas pedal to the mat.

The behemoth increased his speed to stay behind me.

I made a quick right turn down a side street.

The behemoth followed me.

"What do you want?" I shouted at my rearview mirror.

The behemoth continued to follow me.

I made a left turn, not bothering to check traffic. I had to get back to Main Street where I would be able to beat a path to the Police Station.

When I looked at my rearview mirror, I saw the behemoth turning onto the street so I increased my speed as much as possible without trying to kill myself or any innocent bystanders.

"Just one more turn and I'll be there," I prayed as I slowed in order not to crush some pedestrians who were crossing the street in front of me.

Suddenly he was directly behind me and creeping up on my bumper. I felt a nudge. I crushed the gas pedal with my foot and took off spinning my wheels and making a terrible racket.

I took my last turn too fast. I felt the car lift up off of one side as I careened around the last turn before I spotted the Police Station. Then my whole world shook as the car fell back down onto all four wheels

When I looked in my rearview mirror again, there was nothing there. No behemoth was following me. I guess he didn't want to visit the Police Station with me.

I threw the gear into park and raced inside to see if Barry was around so I could tell him about my behemoth.

"Is Barry Johnson here?" I asked breathlessly as I stood in front of the counter that separated the public from the inner workings of the Police Station.

"Yeah, somewhere," answered a distracted officer as he tried to continue his task at hand.

I looked around and finally spotted him off to one side at a corner desk. I waved at him trying to get his attention. He was involved in a conversation that seemed to be holding his complete concentration. I waved again. I didn't want to shout.

Barry finally looked in my direction but his telephone conversation had not ended. He acknowledged me with a nod of his head and proceeded with his conversation. A few seconds later he was up out of his chair and standing in front of me at the counter.

"What's wrong, Ellen?"

"Someone was following me and trying to run me off the road."

"Did you get a license number?"

"No, all I could see in my rearview mirror were the extremely bright headlights of a massively huge vehicle of some kind. It was a dark monster and it wouldn't stop coming at me until I turned down the street heading for the Police Station."

"Let me drive you back to the motel. You leave your car here for the night. I'll get someone to help me bring it to you when I get off work."

"I have to go to work."

"That's fine. I'll have it to you bright and early just as soon as I get off my shift."

"Who do you think is bothering me, Barry? This is getting a little old, you know."

"Yeah, I'm sure it is. I just had a conversation with the Sheriff of Richards County. He tells me that Maggie's son has been in a lot of trouble in that county. Do you know anything about that?"

"No, just what Maggie has told me which isn't much."

"Ellen, I believe your problem is directly related to the disappearance of your friend. Whoever has Maggie might even know you and might be afraid that you'll figure out the puzzle."

"Boy, I wish that was true. I don't have the foggiest idea of who would take Maggie and why?"

"But they don't know that."

"What should I do, Barry? I don't know who is after me and I won't know when I should be afraid unless I have to be afraid all of the time and of everyone I know."

"I'm going to clear it with my boss back there in that office," he said pointing to a corner office where a uniformed officer was sitting at a desk working away at a computer. "Then I'm going to drive you and Nikki back to the motel so you can get some sleep. Your car won't be parked in the lot, so they shouldn't even know you're there. I'll talk to the night manager and tell him not to let anyone know that you're there. You need to call your son and let him know, okay?"

I thought Barry's idea about not parking my car in the motel lot was an excellent idea except – maybe – what if? There seemed to be a little hidden doubt wedged into the back recesses of my mind.

The exception was related to maybe my stalker had already seen my car in the lot the night before and what if he came after me at the motel? If that exception and what if occurred, I wouldn't have a way of getting away from the danger.

"No, Barry, on second thought, I think I need my car with me. I need to know that I have a way to run and go beyond the reaches of the one chasing me."

Barry looked hurt by my objection to his plan, "Are you sure, Ellen?"

"I'm not sure about anything right now. I just want to keep my car close by. You understand, don't you?"

"Yeah, I guess so but I will follow you when you drive to the motel and I'll check your room out. I'll speak to the night manager and tell him to call me if anyone, I don't care who it is, asks for you."

"That's fine, Barry. I would appreciate that."

"Are you calm enough to leave now? Or, do you want to hang around here for a while?"

"I'm really, really tired but I'll stay here until you get a break. Okay?"

"That's good, Ellen. It shouldn't be too long. We're just a little shorthanded tonight. There was an accident on the other end of town and a couple of squad cars are at the scene. At least one of them should be back soon."

I clutched Nikki close to me as I sat down on one of the empty chairs across from the counter. I was planning to people watch.

People watching was another game I played. Unlike Hide and Seek, people watching required no active participation other than the use of my eyes and ever active mind.

Sitting in a police station would expose me to people I would probably never meet anywhere else. I decided people watching was going to be a real treat, one like I had never had before.

Well, I was wrong. People watching is fun when there are people to watch. It seemed that nobody was breaking the law in our little town. No arrests were being made. No forms of screaming, fighting, and/or violent aggression were being displayed for any reason.

That was a good thing, wasn't it? Maybe I'll have a decent night's sleep without any unwanted terror being foisted in my direction.

I was trying to stifle a yawn when Barry caught me in the act.

"Not much longer, Ellen. I know you'd like to get out of here."

"I'm fine, Barry. Just a little tired, that's all."

Five minutes later I was in my car driving toward the motel with Barry following me closely. I glanced up into my rearview mirror and smiled when I saw the reflection of the town police car. It felt good to be protected. It had been so long.

Barry pecked me on the cheek with a goodnight, sleep tight, kiss and went on his way to talk to the night clerk and then go back to work.

I closed the door to my motel room and fell across my bed, fully clothed, while Nikki curled up next to me. We were tired, no doubt about it. The world could have come to an end and I don't think I would have heard it. Even if I did, I probably wouldn't have cared.

My telephone rang.

I didn't answer the noisy disturbance, not at first, because I couldn't figure out what was making the loud sound.

Suddenly the ringing stopped and I slipped back into slumber.

It started again. It was loud and obnoxious and definitely insistent.

"Hello," I whispered softly as I tried to position the receiver next to my ear without sitting up on the bed.

"Ellen, Ellen, help me," said a barely audible voice on the other end of the connection.

"What? I can barely hear you."

"Please, Ellen, help me."

"Is that you, Maggie? Speak a little louder. I can't hear you very well."

"I can't, Ellen. He doesn't know I'm calling you."

"Where are you, Maggie?"

"I don't know."

"Who are you with?"

"I don't know."

"Why are you there?"

"I don't know."

"What's the phone number you're calling from?"

"I don't know."

The line went dead. Silence was all I could hear until the dial tone jarred into place blaring in my ear.

When I woke up the next morning I found the telephone receiver tangled in my bed covers.

"Oh, my God! It wasn't a dream," I screamed as I jerked the receiver from the covers and placed it on its cradle.

I quickly showered, dressed, grabbed Nikki, and checked myself out of the motel. I raced home where I planned to call Barry until I realized that I still didn't know whether my phone was bugged, or not.

"Now what?" I asked Nikki.

I knew Barry wasn't working at that hour of the morning, so my only choice was to call him, if I could find his number in the local telephone directory, and ask for his address so I could drive to his house and tell him about the call during the night from Maggie.

I located a listing for B. Johnson, no address listed, just the name of a subdivision. I dialed the number listed and prayed it was the right B. Johnson.

"Hello," shouted a masculine voice after the sixth ring.

"Barry? Are you Barry Johnson?"

"Who wants to know?" was the gruff response.

"Ellen – Ellen Holcombe."

"Is that you, Ellen? What's wrong? Did something happen?"

"Barry, I need to talk to you. I know you should be getting some sleep so you can go to work, but I need to talk to you. Tell me your address and I'll come to your house. I don't want to say anything important over the telephone."

"Why? What's the matter?"

"Your address, Barry?'

"I'll meet you at the police station in twenty minutes. My place is a mess. I don't want you to see it until I clean it up."

"Sure, okay, twenty minutes?"

"Yeah. Are you sure you can't tell me over the phone?"

"No, I can't. At least, I don't think I can but I'll tell you about it when I see you."

I hung up the telephone and started walking from room to room through my house. I needed to know that my house trasher had not returned.

Nikki was close on my heels trying to look bright eyed and alert as she displayed her tiny protective front.

Everything looked as I had left it the night before but I had the feeling that my entire life was being violated. Something or someone was penetrating all things that were Ellen Holcombe and I didn't like it.

I picked Nikki up from the floor and carried her out the front door to my car. I wanted some answers and I was going to keep searching until I found some.

I waited in the parking lot at the police station. I had the feeling that the people inside the building thought I was becoming a 'frequent flyer', one who reports everything to the police no matter how trivial the problem, or whether or not it was a legal or police matter.

I stroked my dog and focused my mind on what I was going to tell Barry.

There was a peck on my car window and Nikki started barking like she was going to destroy the reason for the disturbance.

I guess I had been so deep in thought that I hadn't noticed Barry's arrival.

"Ellen, are you all right?"

"Yes, Barry, I was just thinking or daydreaming or something like that so I didn't see you pull into the lot."

"You don't want to go inside, do you?" he asked in a voice that told me to say no.

"No, we can talk right here. Why don't you get in my car so it can provide a little more privacy."

I watched Barry as he walked around the front of my car. He looked like he was dragging. His shoulders were sagging and he seemed to have to will his feet to move, one in front of the other.

"Barry, I'm so sorry to bother you. Lord knows you have been pestered to death by me and my problems."

"No – no, Ellen. I want you to call me. I want to help."

"Are you sure? You look so tired."

"A little sleep will cure that. Now, what's wrong? Why couldn't you tell me about it over the phone?"

The dam burst. The pent up tears and frustration flooded from my eyes as I fought to regain my composure.

Nikki climbed up my chest placing her tiny feet on my shoulder as she tried to comfort me.

Barry put his arm around me and pulled himself towards me to help me find some kind of release.

"Give me a minute, Barry," I said between snubs as I tried to get a grip.

"Okay, honey, I'm waiting. No problem. Take your time. We've got the rest of our lives, you know."

I looked at him when he called me honey. I knew then that he was just as vulnerable as I was to the pain of heartbreak.

"I know this is going to sound really stupid, Barry, but you've got to help me understand what is going on," I said as I swallowed back another gush of tearful frustration.

"Nothing you have ever told me has been stupid, Ellen. Get that idea out of your head."

I took a deep breath and began, "I couldn't call you from home because I think my phone is wiretapped. I mentioned the possibility to you before, but I don't think you ever took the time to inspect my telephone box. So much has been going on, I'm sure it slipped your mind."

"Yeah, it did. I'll check it later today. I'm sorry that I forgot about it. What was it that you couldn't tell me over the phone?'

"It's going to sound strange but here goes......

"Last night I stayed at the motel and you already know about that. I was so exhausted from working on the house that I was afraid I wouldn't wake up if something happened."

"Yeah, I know, honey. Did something happen? I told the night clerk to call me if there was a problem," he said angrily.

"I'm not sure, Barry. I heard my phone ringing during the night, I think."

"You think? Didn't you answer it?"

"Not the first time. It took me a few seconds to realize that it was my phone ringing and when I reached over to pick it up, the ringing stopped."

"Maybe you dreamed it."

"That's what I thought, too, until it started ringing a second time."

"Did you answer it?"

"I think I did."

"Who was it?"

"Maggie."

"Maggie Boothe called you last night?"

"I think so."

"Where was she?"

"She didn't tell me. All she could say when I asked her questions was 'I don't know'. She said that over and over again. She said she wanted me to help her, Barry. Maggie needs help and I don't know how to do it."

"Are you sure you didn't dream all of this?"

"No, I'm not sure."

"How would Maggie know where you were? You weren't at home. How could she know you were staying at the motel?"

"I don't know."

"That fact alone should tell you that it must have been a dream."

"Yeah, it should. Except for one thing."

"What's that?"

"When I woke up, the telephone receiver was tangled in my bed covers. I must have talked to someone last night. If it wasn't Maggie, then who was it?"

"Did you recognize the voice? Was it Maggie's?"

"I couldn't tell – not really. She was speaking in a whisper. I could barely hear her."

"It could have been anyone then."

"Yes, it could have. Or maybe it was just a dream. I really don't think it was a dream. I think it happened. It may not have been Maggie that I was talking to but I'm sure I talked to someone. I wish I could remember everything I said or that she said."

"Let's drive over to the motel and see if the night clerk is available."

"He won't be there. He was already gone when I checked out this morning."

"We'll get his name, address, and phone number."

"What is he going to be able to tell us?"

"Whether or not you got a telephone call."

"There is no switchboard. The calls are direct into the room."

"Somebody has to tell the caller which room you're in, don't they?"

"I think there is some kind of recording that lists the names and room numbers. The room number then becomes the last four numbers of the seven digit telephone number. Like my room was 201 so they put a zero in front and added the 988 exchange number. My room telephone number is 988-0201. They do that a lot in hospitals."

"I told the guy not to tell anyone you were here. Your name shouldn't have been on that list."

"Well, they might have seen my car. It was parked right in front. All the caller had to do was dial the room numbers closest to my car."

"What about long distance calls?"

"They have it blocked. You have to dial the operator and bill it to another number such as a calling card or credit card or maybe your home phone number. I think that's how it works. I didn't make any long distance calls so I'm not really sure about the procedure. You can make all the local calls you want at no charge."

"Was there Caller ID on the phone."

"No, I don't think so."

"We'll find that out from the clerk on duty as well as the other information about the night clerk. I want to check and see if anyone was asking about you."

Barry wasn't on duty so he remained in my car as I drove to the motel.

When we arrived at the motel, I grabbed Nikki and followed Barry into the office that was located just inside the front door.

"May I help you?" asked the suited man behind the front desk.

"I need some information," said Barry as he displayed the badge he carried in his wallet.

"Sure thing. What do you need to know?"

"What is the name, address, and phone number for your night clerk?"

"Why? Is there a problem? Did he do something wrong?" sputtered the man whose name tag proclaimed him to be 'John'.

"No, nothing is wrong. I just need to ask him a few questions, that's all."

"His name is David Dent. I'll get the information for you. If you're going to talk to him, I would wait until a little later. I tried to call him a few minutes ago and I didn't get an answer. Is that all you need?" he said as he handed Barry a piece of paper.

"One more thing."

"Okay."

"Is there any way to check to see if any incoming calls were made to Room 201 last night?"

"No, the monthly bills don't list the incoming or outgoing calls if they are local. You need to get that from the phone company. No long distance calls can be charged on the phone. Long distance incoming calls might be listed on the monthly bill. I don't think they are, but I'm not sure; especially since we don't have to pay for them."

Barry turned to leave. He caught a glimpse of a note tucked into the mail slot for Room 201.

"John, there is a note in slot 201. Who is it for?"

The clerk reached for the note and read it before handing it to Barry who also read the note.

"It's for Ellen Holcombe," mumbled John.

"This is Ellen Holcombe," said Barry as he stepped aside to point towards me.

I took the note from Barry and visibly paled a few shades after I had read the handwritten words.

"Do you know who left this note?" demanded Barry.

"No, I found it here on the desk."

"You didn't see the person who left it on the desk?"

"No, it must have happened when I went to the bathroom. I wasn't gone very long, a couple of minutes maybe," explained the flustered clerk.

"Why didn't you give it to Mrs. Holcombe when she checked out?" Barry snapped.

"I didn't know it was here. I didn't know she had checked out."

"Barry, John wasn't here when I checked out. There was someone else back there."

"Was it David?"

"No, it was someone else."

"Must have been the guy that works weekends and fills in for David and me when we have to be out. His name is Frank Arrington. He is a relative of the guy that owns this place."

"Is he here when you usually come to work?"

"No, David is usually here. David must have had to leave early for some reason. When I came in, Frank wasn't here but neither was David. I didn't think anything of it though. David usually goes out the back as soon as he sees me pull into the lot. We barely even speak to each other most of the time."

"So you don't really know who was working?" questioned Barry.

"No, not really."

"What's this Frank Arrington's address and so on? I may need to speak to him about the note."

"Are you going to tell me what this is about?" asked John as he handed the address information for Frank Arrington to Barry.

"You read the note. What do you think this is about?"

"I don't have a clue," sputtered John.

"Neither do we," said Barry as he turned to leave.

He ushered me into the passenger side of the car as I clutched my little Nikki to my breast.

"Give me your keys, Ellen."

"What are you going to do?" I begged.

"The note said they have Eddy. He's your son, isn't he?"

I nodded my head in answer.

"We're going to pay Eddy a visit."

"Then what?"

"Don't know. Let's do this one step at a time. Okay?"

"Okay," was the only word I could force myself to utter.

CHAPTER 10: EDDY, ARE YOU IN THERE?

The drive was longer than I remembered it ever being. He lived in the next town, not the next state. Twenty miles should not take forever.

"Can't you go any faster?" I asked Barry.

"No, not if we want to be alive when we get there. He lives in Ritzland, but where in Ritzland?"

"The other end of town. It's a place called Duran. You know where that is, don't you?"

"Where in Duran?"

"In the trailer park directly across from the bridge. You drive straight into the park from the bridge."

"No problem, I know where that is."

Finally we were crossing the bridge, entering the trailer park.

"Which mobile home?"

"Drive to the end of this road and turn left. It's the first trailer on the left."

"I see a car. Is that his?"

"Yeah, he must be home."

I jumped out of the car and ran to Eddy's front door where I pounded on it with a closed fist.

"Eddy, Eddy, are you in there?" I screamed while flailing away at the door.

The door did not open nor did it buckle under my physical abuse.

"Barry, he's not answering the door," I screamed.

"Yeah, I can see that. Do you have a key?"

"Yes, sure. Eddy gave it to me so I would be able to get in if it became necessary. I'll get it. It's in my handbag in the car," I said as I raced back to the car and dumped the contents of my handbag onto the front seat.

"Slow down, Ellen."

"I can't. What if someone hurt him? I'll kill them, Barry. I swear to God I'll kill them if they hurt one single hair on his head."

"We don't know that, Ellen. Calm down."

"Here it is. I found the key," I said as I handed it to Barry with my trembling hands.

Barry shoved the key into the lock.

"Step back, Ellen. Let me check inside first."

I looked at him with my mouth hanging open and stepped back as he instructed.

Barry turned the lock and threw the door open quickly as he, too, stepped aside to avoid what? A bullet? A fist?

Nothing came flying out of the door so we both cautiously entered the aged, but well cared for, mobile home.

Unlike his brother Aaron, Eddy was a neat freak. Everything had a place and everything was in its place every hour of every day.

"Your son lives here?"

"Yes."

"Alone?"

"Yes. Why?"

"I've never seen such a neat and tidy place with only a man on the premises."

"He's always been a neat nut. So this is just his normal way of keeping his place in shape," I answered with an embarrassed smile.

"You stay here, Ellen. I'm going to go down the hall and check the rest of the place out."

I stood, impatiently waiting, for the 'all clear' before following him down the hall to find my son. I heard the sound of a car driving slowly through the trailer park. I glanced to see the occupant of the vehicle and my mind registered a person that I should know but there wasn't time to focus on that driver, especially because it wasn't Eddy.

"He's not here. No one is here, Ellen."

"He doesn't go anywhere without his car. He's got to be here somewhere."

"Ellen, come here and look for yourself," he said as he pointed down the dark, narrow hallway. "Does he have any close friends here in this trailer park?"

"No, he's a loner, has been since he was a teenager. He never was very close to anybody after that because they would take advantage of him. He used to be such a trusting soul until one friend too many stole his cassette tapes of the metallic hard rock bands that he used to play all the time."

"Well, he's not here now. Look for a note or some kind of sign that will tell you why he's gone."

"Okay, but you can see there is nothing in the living room. I'll try his bedroom."

The bedroom was immaculate so I traveled onto the bathroom. It was what Eddy would consider a mess. The traces of foam shave cream and tiny hairs from his dark brown, almost black, beard had dried onto the sink. The razor had been thrown onto the back of the toilet and Eddy's wallet was on the floor next to the toilet bowl.

"Barry, come here quick!" I screamed as my heart raced from mounting panic.

"Don't touch anything, Ellen. This might turn out to be a crime scene after all."

"Oh my God, Barry, I didn't want him involved in this mess. Who in the world would take him from me? Why?"

I cried as my panic melted away and was replaced by a mother's worry.

"Stop it, Ellen. You've got to calm down and think. Do you understand me?" Barry asked me as he held me firmly by placing each of his hands on my upper arms and squeezing me so that I would feel a little pain and look at him.

"Why would they take Eddy?" I pleaded.

"That's what I want you to think about, Ellen."

"It's me they are after, me and Maggie. We are the ones who were checking out the comings and goings at the little house across the street. They already have Maggie. Why would they want to take Eddy? Why didn't they take me?"

"I don't know, babe. Maybe they just couldn't take a chance on grabbing you because I've been hanging around. Maybe the person who has Eddy isn't involved with anything you're doing. He's not into anything illegal, is he?"

"No, no, of course not. You couldn't get any more straight laced and honest than Eddy. He doesn't even drive his car fast. Oh, he dabbled in things he shouldn't have when he was a teenager but he got over all of that."

"What kind of things?"

"Typical teenage stuff. Drinking was the hardest thing for him to quit, but he did. He smoked pot a few times and even grew some from seeds, but that was something he didn't want to get into too deeply. Number one, he couldn't afford the junk. The second thing was that all of his problems were still there after he came down from the drug high or sobered up from the alcohol. I'm glad he learned his lessons. A lot of kids don't learn."

"How long ago was the drug thing?"

"Let's see now. He's thirty-three so it's got to be about fifteen years."

"That shouldn't be the reason, but you never know."

"I do. I know it isn't drugs," I said emphasizing my faith in my son with the tone of my voice.

"If not drugs, what else could he be into?"

"Nothing, that's just it. Eddy leads a very solitary, passive life. He doesn't like to make waves, but he will if he has to defend himself."

"Look around and see if you see any kind of note from Eddy or the person that took him away from here."

"It's me; me and my snooping. I'm going to get my baby killed," I sputtered as I tried to search for clues.

"Ellen, don't worry. We'll find him. Okay?" consoled Barry as he placed his comforting arms around his new and best friend, Ellen Holcombe. I sobbed against his strong chest until there were no more salty tears left to roll down my sagging cheeks.

"Let's go, hon, there isn't anything here that gives us any kind of a clue."

We walked out to the car where I was faced with the problem of driving the car. I didn't know if I could manage that task. The look on my face must have told Barry exactly what I was thinking.

"Give me your keys, Ellen. You're in no shape to drive."

I handed them over gladly and walked around to the passenger side of the vehicle where my wonderful friend, Barry Johnson, opened the door and helped me into my seat.

"Thanks, Barry. I didn't know if I could drive."

Barry nodded his head in agreement and closed the car door gently.

"Ellen, we're going to my house. You'll have to forgive the mess. I am a male living all alone in a space that is only there for the purpose of eating and sleeping. Once you get over the shock of seeing the place, I want you to make yourself at home because that's where you are going to be living for a few days."

"I can't do that, Barry."

"Why not?"

"What if Eddy tries to reach me?"

"We'll go to your house later and forward your calls to this phone."

"What if he comes to my door?"

"I can't do anything about that. If you leave him a note, the person who is doing all of this will know where you are staying. Your son would try to call, wouldn't he?"

"Sure, if he can. I still can't stay here."

"Now why?"

"What would people think?"

"That you have entered the twenty first century and are trying out the latest model," said Barry with an evil grin.

"Barry, I don't believe you!" I gasped as I joined his laughter for the moment.

Well, Barry was right. His place was a mess. Now I knew what his real reason for my staying with him was. He wanted help in cleaning up. He wanted the touch of a woman in his home and I was proud to say that I was going to be that woman.

CHAPTER 11: MISSING MADNESS

"Barry?" I said as I sat on the sofa admiring Barry's house now that it was presentable to non-dwellers.

"Yeah?"

"Did you see a car drive by Eddy's house while we were there?"

"No, was it somebody you knew?"

"Well, I didn't at the time. You were just going into Eddy's trailer and you had your gun drawn. That little movement alone distracted me so much that it wasn't until just now that I remembered who I saw driving the car."

"Who was it?"

"It was Marty, Maggie's son. He seemed to be driving really slow and trying not to look at what we were doing. I just barely caught him with the corner of my eye. It took a while for my brain to finally filter the information down to where I could remember it. I'm now sure it was him. I didn't know that he and Eddy were friends. There was no reason they shouldn't be friends except that there was an age difference and they hung with different crowds."

"Do you trust Marty?"

"I have no reason not to, Barry. He's Maggie's son and I would trust Maggie with my life."

"Have you had any contact with Marty?"

"Not recently, why do you ask?"

"We questioned him about his mother's disappearance and we haven't heard from him since talking to the police department, I mean. Seems to be a little cold, don't you think?"

"I don't know what to think, not anymore," I answered with a sigh. "Maggie, my best friend in all the world, and now my son are missing. Why? Is it something I did or didn't do?"

"Ellen, you can't blame yourself."

"Why not? Who can I blame?"

"I don't really know except you can't blame yourself. Do you understand me?"

"Sure, I do. All I want is for us or anyone to find Maggie and Eddy. And – I want to do it soon," I answered as I fought back the sudden wave of tears that were bordering on the edge of my eyelids.

"Now, about Marty. Why wouldn't he be concerned about his mother's disappearance? Maybe he knows something that we don't. Ellen, you and I should go track down that unconcerned young man and find out why he is taking everything that is happening all around him so lightly."

"Well, I guess the first place to start looking would be where Marty lives. Do you have the address? If you don't, I have it in my book in my handbag."

"Yeah, I should have it written somewhere in my pocket notebook," Barry answered as he started flipping through the pages of information he had gathered on the case.

"You certainly have a lot of notes, Barry. Is there anything in there that I should know about?"

"Naw, most of this information came from you. Grab your handbag, Ellen. We're going to go pay Marty a visit right now."

"Don't you have to work?"

"I am working. Trying to keep you out of trouble is a full time job," Barry said with a smile.

I was becoming more comfortable with Barry with each passing moment. It felt good, really good, to be looked after, and watched over after so many months of being alone, except for Nikki, that is.

Speaking of Nikki, where is she?

I had brought her with me and she had entered Barry's house perched on my chest and hugged close to me with my arms. Nikki didn't like change, not normally, but entering Barry's house didn't seem to bother her, not one, single, little, bit. As soon as I placed her onto the floor, she started exploring the place, giving it the once over, sniffing in every corner and under every chair until she accepted what she found without much fuss.

I knew my little girl dog was tired of being moved from one place to another while all of the "missing madness" was taking place, but I was afraid to leave her home alone. I was afraid someone would take it upon themselves to hurt her. I couldn't have that. I couldn't allow anyone to hurt my Nikki.

"Barry, do you know where Nikki might be?"

"Yeah, she seems to have attached herself to my bedroom. Come here and take a look."

I rose from the chair with my handbag straps strung over my arm and walked to where Barry was looking into another room from the small hall.

Nikki was centered perfectly on Barry's bed pillow with her tiny body circled into a little round ball. She was so soundly asleep that she didn't hear us at the doorway.

"You know, Barry, I was always told that if a dog likes you, you must be a good person. It appears that you have passed Nikki's inspection with flying colors, doesn't it?"

Barry lifted my chin and planted a warm, gentle kiss on my lips.

"I believe that's the nicest thing a woman has ever said to me," he said with a silly grin plastered from ear to ear. "Now, we'd better get going before I decide that I need a little more than a kiss."

"Nikki, wake up, girl. Let's hit the road."

I wasn't sure I wanted to leave. Going beyond the kiss sounded good to me, too.

The drive was short because Marty lived about five blocks from Barry's house.

One half of the two family house was empty, no renters, and the side where Marty lived was empty of any human dwellers. The only life form that we could see from peeking through the windows was a cat that looked very hungry and very angry.

"It looks like Marty hasn't been home for a while," I said as I whispered to Barry while peeking through the kitchen window. "I know it was him that I saw earlier today at Eddy's house, but he doesn't seem to be living here, does he?"

"No, he hasn't been here for a while. Do you know if there is a spare key hidden around the place?"

"Are you going to go inside?"

"Yes, I was thinking about feeding the cat."

"That's a good idea. Let's do that, Barry. That cat really looks hungry, don't you think?"

I wasn't worried about a starving cat. Not really. All I wanted to do was get inside to see if we could find a trail to Maggie, Eddy, and now Marty.

I looked under the flower pot that contained the remains of what looked to be a geranium if it had lived. Nothing. The welcome mat was tattered around the edges and almost fell apart when I pulled it up from the front stoop. Again, nothing, no key.

Barry searched the ledge over the front door by feeling around with his fingers. Nothing except dirt and grime. We both started walking around the side of the house. The windows were too high off the ground for us to search along the top, but Barry could just barely reach the lower ledge of the frame. Once again, nothing – no key.

We continued to walk towards the back of the house.

"Barry, I'm getting a bad feeling about this."

"What kind of a bad feeling?"

"I don't have specifics, just a bad feeling in my gut. You know what I mean."

"Yeah, I do."

We searched every nook and cranny in and around the back door to no avail. Then I spotted a brick under the wooden step that led up to the back door.

"Barry, maybe it's under that brick."

"What brick?"

"Under this step. You can barely see, let alone reach it."

"Here, let me get down there to see," he said as he quickly lowered himself to his knees and crawled close enough to the step to reach under it.

"I hope it's there."

"No, no, I don't see anything on the ground. I don't feel anything on the ground except the bugs. Wait a minute. Look! There is something attached to the bottom of the brick."

Barry was holding the brick in front of both of us. There was a really dirty plastic sandwich bag folded over many times around a small object and the plastic bag was glued to the brick.

"That's it, Barry. That must be the key."

Barry struggled with the brick trying to pull the plastic bag from its secured position. It was tearing but it was a tiny bit at a time coming loose from the glue. He pulled a pocket knife from his trouser pocket and started cutting the plastic fiercely. So much for being nice and gentle.

"It's a key, all right. I hope it's the right key. This thing has been here a long time. Hopefully the locks haven't been changed."

Barry pushed the key into the slot of the back door lock. Slowly he turned the key and I stood next to him with my eyes focused directly on his hand that seemed to have a slight tremble.

"It's going to open, Ellen. Stand back in case the cat springs at us. Frightened cats will do that, you know."

I stepped back for a moment to ease his mind. Then I moved forward again appearing to be his clinging shadow.

We entered the kitchen and caught a whiff of an overused cat litter box. We didn't see the litter box but we could surely smell it. On the floor in front of the sink there were several small empty bowls that must have contained cat food at one time. At least, Marty was trying to make sure his cat didn't die of starvation. Another plastic container had a drop or two of water in the bottom.

"Barry, I'm going to look into the cabinet to see if there is any cat food. Is that okay?"

"Sure, that's why we came in here, isn't it?"

As I started tugging at cabinets, Barry proceeded through the house with his gun drawn. He wasn't going to take any chances whatsoever.

A minute or so later, he returned to the kitchen.

"Nothing is wrong in the rest of the house except that Marty's housekeeping is nowhere near as good as your son, Eddy's. Marty lives more like me," he said with a smile. "How's the kitty cat doing?"

"Just fine. She just needed some food, water, and attention. She's very friendly."

"I'd be friendly, too, if someone was finally going to feed me," he said as he reached down to stroke the cat's back as she gulped her food. "Is there any more food?"

"Yes."

"Well, you maybe should put some more of it down for her. Who knows when Marty will return?"

"He must care for her. He obviously didn't want her to starve. Look at all of the dirty empty bowls. I spotted some cat litter in that small pantry. I will change the box so she won't have such a mess to scratch in. It will certainly improve the smell of the place."

"Okay, but hurry, Ellen. I want to get a bulletin out on the missing Marty and Eddy, too, and check on any information about Maggie."

It took about five minutes to clean up the cat litter box and stow the garbage bag into the trunk of Barry's car for disposal when we arrived at the proper place, either his or mine.

Nikki greeted us both with excited enthusiasm when we reached the car. I had left her sitting on the front seat for safety reasons. I didn't want her to be hurt while Barry and I prowled around Marty's house.

"Ellen, I'm going to drop you at my house and then I'm going into work. I need to do some things, and I need to do them pretty quickly."

"That's fine. As a matter of fact, I'm going to go to my house since it's daylight and check on my stuff, if you think that's okay?"

"It should be, especially since it is broad daylight. But, don't take any chances, okay Ellen? Promise me you won't take any chances?"

"I promise. If anything looks amiss, I'll scream bloody murder," I said as I winced when I thought about my choice of words.

CHAPTER 12: THE ESSENCE

I actually enjoyed the drive from Barry's house to my house. It was nice to be alone; sounds silly doesn't it after I complained so much about being alone all the time. Believe it or not, I had gotten used to being alone and whether I liked it or not, it was a part of my life that I strangely missed. I guess it was the space, the one on one feeling that I had with Nikki. I could express all of my feelings, right or wrong, and Nikki wouldn't argue with me. She would allow me to say what I wanted to say, usually without interrupting me. Only if she had a sudden nature call did she dare voice her opinion with an insistent bark.

"Home, Nikki. Isn't it wonderful to see?"

I carefully lifted Nikki to the ground and exited the car. I couldn't wait to get inside so I could be surrounded by my things. I wanted to be able to take off my clothes and run around in my bra and panties and not be embarrassed about the width of my backside. Nikki didn't care if it was a few sizes too large. To tell you the truth, I didn't care either. At least, I knew where my backside was and where it belonged. Unlike Maggie, Eddy, and Marty, I was at home basking in the pleasure of Nikki's company.

I approached the front door like someone returning from a long vacation with only the desire to insert the key into the lock, turn it quickly, and rush inside to see the bounty of my life.

I pulled back the storm door and found a hole where my lock had been located.

"Whoa, Nikki. Something's wrong here. Someone has been inside."

I closed the storm door and picked Nikki up and held her close to me.

"Girl, I'm going to put you in the car. If someone is still in there, I don't want you getting hurt. Okay, girl?" I said as I planted a gentle kiss to the top of her head as I walked back to my car where I slowly placed her on the car seat in the front on the passenger side. I made sure I had my keys because I was going to lock her inside out of harm's way.

I looked around the front yard and glanced down the side of the house but I could see nothing that was out of place. The only evident sign of unwanted visitors was the missing lock and I didn't see that problem until I opened the storm door.

I decided to walk to the back door and see if there was a lock missing from that door. I trudged through the high damp grass until I reached the steps that led up to the door. I knew the steps creaked from applied weight at times so I stepped softly and slowly onto the first wooden tread. When I stepped up to the second step, I could hear the creak, but it wasn't as loud as it usually was.

"Sh-sh-sh," I whispered to myself as if that were going to quiet the creak.

I stepped onto the third step quickly and almost jumped to the fourth step that was the top of the small deck that was outside my back door. I pulled at the storm door and saw that this lock was intact. No destruction had been wielded against that mechanism that prevented entrance into my world.

I inserted the key and entered into my kitchen.

All looked at peace with the world in my little kitchen. Nothing looked out of place, no appliances had been tossed from the counter, and no cabinets had been emptied onto the clean floor. But, I could feel the essence of the person or persons who had entered my home uninvited. Maybe they weren't still there in body, but some of their spirit had remained to linger and had infiltrated into my domain. Goose bumps raised on my arms as I left the kitchen and entered the living room.

On the wall in the living room, above my sofa, spray painted in blood red letters were the words:

NO COPS OR NO MAGGIE, EDDY, AND MARTY.

My hand went to my mouth as I screamed as loud as I could. I knew no one would come running to help me. I was alone. Remember, I wanted to be alone, I was so happy that I would be alone.

When I finally shut my mouth and caused the noise to cease, I looked around some more to see if I could find any more messages.

None of this made sense to me. If the people doing this had been watching me at all, they would know that the cops were already involved. Barry is a cop. He was investigating this whole mess.

Again, nothing looked out of place, but I felt as if my whole life had been turned upside down and they had pilfered through everything that I owned.

I opened my dresser drawer that contained my nightgowns and panties and I felt as if every piece of clothing had been moved and then placed back into its former position except that it was slightly off maybe a fraction of an inch. Perhaps that was my writer's imagination working overtime, but it was something I truly believed.

I went back to my front door, opened it, and ran to my car of get my little Nikki.

"Come on, girl. It's all clear for the time being."

I returned to the front door and inspected it trying to see if I could figure out how they removed the lock.

"Looks to me like they used some kind of small saw and cut completely around the entire mechanism. It had been cut closely, very closely, to the mechanism and that was all of the damage that was inflicted upon the door. Nikki, whoever did this has done this kind of thing before. They certainly did a really neat job."

Nikki walked around the house and sniffed at everything her little nose could reach. She, too, felt the essence of someone who didn't belong in our world.

Suddenly I had the need to check on the little white house across the street. I walked to my living room window, standing back a bit, so it would be harder to see me from the other side.

"It's got something to do with that house, Nikki. I know that deep down in my heart, it's got something to do with that house."

I watched the house focusing in on the front windows over which the blinds were closed allowing no sight line inside to their world of mystery.

"Nikki, someone is in there looking back at me," I said as I stepped further back from the window. I couldn't see that someone, but I knew he or she was in there watching me.

I looked around me inside my living room. Was there a camera inside my house? Had they infiltrated my world and invaded my privacy completely?

"Okay, Nikki, we are looking for alien invaders. Let's go, girl."

I fetched a flashlight from the kitchen, then I lowered my old, tired, body to the floor to Nikki's level and started shining the flashlight into every hidden corner, under every chair and table. I was looking for a bug whether it would be a camera or a listening device, I had no idea. All I knew was, if there was something strange planted in my house, I was going to find it and destroy it.

I thought the kitchen or the living room would be the best place to plant the device. In my house it most definitely would be the living room. I didn't tend to spend a lot of time in the kitchen cooking for me.

I looked in the heat and air conditioning vent, at the top and bottom of each table lamp, inside the drawers of the end tables that contained only accumulated junk. I actually turned the sofa over and explored the gauze webbing that covered the inner parts of the seat. It looked as if the original staples were in place and had not been tampered with.

Then it occurred to me that I had to find a way to close my front door. It was evident that I would need to purchase a new door to replace the damaged one so I decided to nail the front door in the closed position until I had a chance to get it repaired. Fortunately, I had a hammer and a few extra-long nails that were my tools for locking out intruders.

I'm sure Nikki thought I was totally losing my mind, but she accepted anything and everything I did. Her only observable objection was to the noise of the pounding hammer.

With that task accomplished, I proceeded to inspect the remaining rooms for any alien invaders.

I looked under the beds, checked the light fixtures, took the drawers from the dressers and chests before turning the skeleton over to inspect the bottom. Nothing, I could find nothing that would prove to me that I was being watched or, at the very least, being listened to.

"Nikki, I can't find anything. How about you, girl? Did you track anything important?" I asked with a smile when I saw her walk into the bedroom stretching her tiny muscles from the sleep she must have been enjoying.

I walked back to the living room and stared at the message that had been painted on my wall. Whoever did this must have known I would not be popping in on him to interrupt his work in progress. I decided to call Barry and read this malarkey to him.

"I would like to speak to Officer Barry Johnson," I said to the gruff sounding man who had answered the telephone.

"Hold on," he shouted into the telephone nearly bursting my eardrum.

I pulled the receiver away from my ear and waited. I could hear blurred voices but no one was holding the telephone. I could hear no sounds of breathing on the other end of the line to signify that the receiver was in anyone's hands.

"Nikki, he must have laid the receiver down on the counter. I bet he's forgotten about me. God knows how long it will be before anyone picks the receiver up to replace it on the cradle," I mumbled angrily to a little dog that didn't care about my problem except that it was interfering with my ability to sit in my easy chair and hold her tiny body.

"Hey, you, Cop!" I shouted loudly into the telephone.

I continued to hear only background noise that was indistinguishable.

"Hey! Is anybody there?" I shouted even louder than the first time.

"Ellen, is that you?"

"Barry, did that cop forget I was on the line?"

"He must have. There isn't anyone standing close to this phone."

"How can a cop be so stupid? What if I was trying to report a crime which is what I'm trying to do right now?"

"Crime? What crime? Is there something new?"

"My secret admirer has left me a message. Do you want me to read it to you?"

"Sure, what is it? Where is it? Did you find it at your house?"

153

"It says "NO COPS OR NO MAGGIE, EDDY, AND MARTY" and it is written the loveliest bright red shade of paint on my living room wall," I said sarcastically because it had been so difficult to reach him. "Also, the lock in my front door has been cut completely out. They didn't bother to try to pick the lock. I guess it was easier to remove it."

"You're kidding?"

"I wish I were, Barry. Do I have your attention now?" I said not too sweetly.

"Okay, okay, Ellen. Don't blame me for the long wait. I didn't even know you were on the line."

"Oh really? Then why did you say 'Ellen, is that you?'"

"Just a hunch, that's all. I'll be over there as soon as I can. It's been really crazy here. I can't leave just now."

"Sure, no problem. I've nailed the front door to the facing, so you'll have to come around to the back if you want to get into the house."

"All right. See you soon Ellen. I've got to go."

I hung up the telephone and wanted to throw something. I couldn't understand why my problem wasn't important enough to make the effort of checking out the message. After all, the lives of three people were threatened, not to mention mine. One of those three missing people was my son and I wanted him back.

"Nikki, what am I going to do?" I cried as I rocked my little dog in my arms.

CHAPTER 13: I'M LOSING IT

When the pity party that I had participated in came to an end, I jumped to my feet, grabbed Nikki, and walked out my back door with my keys in hand. I was going to do some of my own investigating.

I was beginning to think that I was becoming a bother to Barry. If that were true, I was going to change things starting right now.

I crossed the street to the little white house that I believed was the root of all of my problems. There was no hesitation in my step, only in my mind. I climbed up the steps that were located at the back of the house but were fronted on my street.

"Is anybody home?" I shouted as I beat on the door with my closed fist. I continued to beat on the door until my abused hand sent signals to my brain indicating that I should stop or else.

Nikki held her body stiff against me not wishing to provoke me in any way. When I heard a soft yelp from her I realized I was holding her too tightly.

155

"I'm sorry, Nikki," I said as I stopped beating on the door. "I didn't mean to squeeze you. We need to go around the house and beat on the back, I mean front, door. Maybe somebody will get the message."

Again, my stride was proud and forceful even though fear was chipping away at my resolve.

I switched Nikki from one arm to the other and proceeded to pound on that door and shouting, "Hey, come to the door. Let me know what you want. Tell me where my son is. Tell me what you've done with Maggie and Marty. I swear I won't talk to the cops, not any more, if you will let me have my son back," I said as I tried to stop the crying that my anger had forced to my eyes causing the flooding tears to stream down my face.

"A rock, Nikki, I need a rock," I said as I started searching through the tall grass, kicking at it with my foot. I spotted a small stone and snatched up it. I stretched my arm back and let the stone fly directly at one of the blind covered windows.

My jaw dropped as I saw the stone bounce off of the glass.

"What the hell?" I asked in disbelief.

"Another rock, I need another rock," I said as I kicked at the grass again and again trying the see through the tears.

A car door slammed and I became silent.

"Nikki, where did that sound come from?"

Nikki wiggled slightly and snuggled closer to me as if she were trying to console me in her own little Chihuahua way.

"A weapon, I need a weapon," I whispered as I raised my searching eyes from the grass to areas where I might find a two by four or something.

"Mrs. Holcombe?"

I spun around at the sound of my name.

"What?"

"We would like to ask you some more questions?"

"Who are you?" I asked as I struggled to place the name to the familiar face that was shining before me.

"Agent Thompson and Agent Chandler and we spoke with you yesterday. You remember, don't you?"

"Of course I remember you," I sputtered as I tried to hide my embarrassment. "I must have been having one of those senior moments you hear people my age talk about so much."

"Is there a problem, Mrs. Holcombe?"

"What do you mean?"

"You threw a rock at that house? Why did you do that?"

"How long have you been here watching me?"

"Not long. As I said, we need to ask you some more questions."

"If I knew anything about this house and anybody who lived here, I wouldn't be throwing a rock at the window trying to get somebody to answer my questions," I said as I tried to control myself and not reach out and smack him down to the ground which was exactly what I wanted to do.

"You are vandalizing this house," said Agent Chandler smugly.

"Arrest me," I sputtered.

"We would rather not. Why don't you just walk across the street and invite us into your house so we can ask you those questions?"

"I won't throw any more rocks. But I don't want either one of you in my house. We can go stand in the middle of the street, for all I care, so you can ask me those questions for which I have no answers."

Agent Thompson took a step towards me with his hand extended as if he were going to take my arm and lead me away from the little white house.

"Don't touch me now or ever," I snapped.

"Mrs. Holcombe, Ellen, please cooperate. We don't want to have to arrest you."

"For what? I'm the only one still around. Everyone else is missing."

"What are you talking about, Ellen?"

"Forget about it. I'm not going to tell you anything I'm sure you already know."

"You're mistaken, Ellen. If we knew everything, we wouldn't need to ask you any questions."

"Sure you do. You don't know how much I know."

"Have you seen any one at the little white house across the street?"

"Do you mind giving me a time reference? Perhaps I should go back in my memory from the time I moved here to my house?"

"What seems to be the problem, Ellen, Mrs. Holcombe?"

"Nothing, I don't know anything about anybody or anything. Now, would you please leave?" I said as I fought back the urge to reach out and bang their heads together, a move that you would see in cartoons.

I don't know why I was talking to the FBI like I was not afraid of them. That's not my thing, being a bully, I mean. I've always been very cooperative and polite with the desire to assist with a problem wherever and whenever I can.

Not today, for some reason I didn't want to cooperate at all with Agents Thompson and Chandler. I didn't trust them, not only because they said they worked for the government, but also for reasons I couldn't quite figure out.

Agent Thompson started to step away but spun around suddenly and put his face directly into my face. We were nearly nose to nose and I didn't like that scene one little bit.

"Have you heard about the bank robbery in Bluefield, Virginia, that happened a couple of months ago?"

"Which one? There seems to have been a rash of them in the last few months?"

"The one that netted the thieves several hundred thousand dollars."

"I heard about one that happened during an armored car delivery. Is it that bank robbery? If it was, more than several hundred thousand dollars was taken. It was more like a million, wasn't it? Wasn't there some gold and jewelry involved? It was all being hauled by one armored truck. That's what I heard through the grapevine. Nothing describing the haul was ever actually printed in the newspapers." I had not paused after any of the questions for him to answer. I knew there wouldn't be an answer, not from him.

"I can't specifically say."

"What about it? Are you guys investigating it? Is that what the interest in the little white house across the street is about?"

"We aren't at liberty to discuss any of the details."

"Sure, right, I know. You can't tell me anything."

"Well, Ellen, have you seen any of the inhabitants of that house recently?" Agent Thompson said as he smiled sweetly in condescension.

"No, I haven't, Agent Thompson."

"Are you sure?"

"Yes, I'm sure. Why should it matter so much? I really haven't seen anybody there unless you count the times that I just feel like somebody's in there. I haven't seen anyone, absolutely no one. I have seen no stray cars that didn't appear to belong in this area except yours. Now, if you don't mind, I would like to take my dog and myself home where we can get some rest. I'm getting tired of standing here on the street."

"All right for now, Mrs. Holcombe. We will more than likely be back."

"I hope not," I whispered as I walked away from the street down the side of the house towards my back door.

I heard the car engine start up and the car sped away as if driven by an angry man that was acting like a petulant child because he didn't get his way.

"Nikki, I think I made him mad," I said as I stifled a laugh.

When the car had driven out of sight, I walked back to the street where I checked my mailbox and then checked the mailbox that was in place for the inhabitants of the little white house across the street.

"Occupant, resident, occupant, doesn't anyone have a name?" I mumbled as I mixed the junk mail with mine and carried in back to my back door and into my house. "Nikki, do you think the government will get me for tampering with the U.S. Mail?"

Nikki didn't have an answer and neither did I.

Suddenly I had the need to look inside of Maggie's mailbox. Back out of the house I ran with the thought that there might be a clue of some kind sequestered in that small black metal box. I knew Maggie wouldn't mind me snooping in her personal life as long as I was trying to help find her and bring her back home along with her son and my son.

The mail had not been retrieved from her mailbox for several days, so there was an accumulation of some of the same type of junk mail that I had retrieved from the mailbox that I shouldn't have been pilfering through. Actually, some of the mail from Maggie's mailbox was older in appearance than the mail from the 'other' mailbox.

"Nikki, I wonder who has been retrieving the mail from the 'other' box? I've never seen anyone get the mail, but that doesn't mean a whole lot because I work for a living."

"Oh, God, now I'm talking to a dog that isn't even there. I left her in the house. I really think I'm losing it. I need to get a life."

CHAPTER 14: NIKKI AND INVESTIGATING

I didn't go back to Barry's house that night. I chose to stay at home in my own bed to worry about my own problems alone except for my little Nikki. Sleep wasn't easy for me because I was waiting for the person who cut my lock out of the front door to come back and finish the job, whatever that might be.

I had opened every piece of Maggie's mail and found nothing I could use. I had pulled and tugged at every little scrap of paper from the 'other' mailbox and I could find nothing again.

I was going to find out who had taken everyone that was near and dear to me if it was the last thing I ever did. That might not be so bad, I mean the last thing I ever did, because I wouldn't want to face the world day after day not knowing why they were gone? If they were still alive? Why were they taken?

Barry had called but I didn't want to talk. The conversation was short and strained so he said goodnight.

Nikki and I were up early the next morning. We were investigating, if that's what you want to call it.

I decided to pose as the people who lived in the house across the street. I went to a pay phone and called the telephone company.

"The phone is giving me problems. I can't seem to be able to make a call. My address is 302 Valleyview Street. I'm using a pay phone at the convenience store down the street. The what? You want the phone number?" A crackling, staticky sound could be heard emanating from my hands as I crumpled cellophane paper near the telephone receiver. "9 crackle-crackle-crackle. Did you get that? What did you say?" Crackle, crackle, crackle continued into the receiver. "This is hopeless. There's something wrong with this phone, too." I said as I hung up the receiver disconnecting the line.

I reached for more change and called the Electric Power Company.

"I am moving into the house at 302 Valleyview Street and I need to get the power changed into my name."

"You need to come into the local office and complete the necessary paperwork, ma'am. We can't help you without a deposit and a release from the party under whose name the utility is listed."

"Since when did you start doing that?"

"It's a policy that's been in effect for a couple of years."

"If I can get Jonathan Smith to call you, will that be enough?"

"We would need the account number."

"Okay, I will contact Mr. Smith. He doesn't live here locally. It may take a while to reach him."

"Yes ma'am."

I hung up the receiver with a sigh.

"Well, that didn't work," I mumbled.

The Town of Stillwell Waterworks was the next victim.

"I don't have any water pressure and there is a puddle of water in my front yard. It hasn't rained. I think there may be a water break. I live at 302 Valleyview Street. Can you send someone out to check this out?"

"Yes ma'am, I will dispatch a truck to your location as soon as possible.

"Thank you," I said as I hung up the receiver.

"We did it, Nikki. The water people are on their way." I said with a smile.

I was so happy about finally, fi-nal-ly, getting somebody to pay attention to my falsehood that I very nearly skipped like a playful child on my way to my car. I know my little dog could feel the change in my attitude as the good mood coursed through my body and almost like an electrical transfer into her small frame.

"We've got to go home and wait, Nikki. I definitely want to be there when they pull up to the door and start pounding on it to find out who had made the phony service call. Then, as an observant, attentive neighbor I want to investigate the investigators, " I smiled as I realized I was having a full adult conversation again with my dog. "If people saw me constantly talking to you, Nikki, they would probably lock me up. Don't tell on me please, girl."

A couple of hours passed as I started my vigil of watching and waiting at my front window, I saw a white truck with "Town of Stillwell" boldly emblazoned on its side.

"They're here, Nikki. Come here, come here, and I'll hold you so you can see what's going on, too."

One burley looking man clad in a work uniform sauntered up to the back door as it faced my house and knocked. He kept looking around the yard for signs of water leaks but saw nothing but dry, parched grass. The day was warm and I'm sure his temper was heating up to match the outside heat. The knocking on the door turned to pounding and shouting as the town employees, now there were two of them standing side by side, tried to ferret out the crank caller.

Suddenly I felt the neighborly need to go outside and approach the house presenting myself as a concerned citizen. I carried Nikki in my arms as I walked out my back door, around my house to my front porch. After a few moments of obvious watching, I strolled to the sidewalk that led to the mysterious little white house across the street.

"Gentlemen, are they not answering?" I asked sweetly.

"No ma'am, do you know the people that live here?" shouted the burley man while his skinny sidekick stood by watching.

"Why, I'm not sure anyone lives there. Do you have a name? I can tell you whether they have moved away or not. Perhaps the house is being rented out to someone new."

"Jonathan Smith owns the house according to our records."

"Yes, I understand that is what is on record at the court house. Yet, I've never seen Mr. Jonathan Smith nor has anyone lived in that house been named Jonathan Smith. I could be wrong, mind you. I don't find it absolutely necessary to keep track of all of the goings on in that house," I said with a smugness on my face that anyone who knew me would laugh at.

"Do you know who might have called about a water leak?"

"I'm sorry, sir. Like I said, I don't think anyone lives there now."

"The bills get paid every month, ma'am, and there has been some water usage. So somebody stays inside long enough to consume enough water for an average family of four."

"You don't say?"

"Are you sure you don't know who lives here?"

"No sir. I haven't seen anyone go in or out of this place since the last couple moved out several days ago. I'm sorry, I take that back. I did see a police officer go inside one day. He only stayed a few minutes and then he continued on his way."

"Did you recognize the police officer?"

"No sir, I really couldn't tell whether it was a man or a woman. I just saw the backside from a distance. I just assumed it was a man from the muscular build."

"Well, we're going to have to write this up as a crank call. My partner here checked the water meter and it looks normal, not running too fast or too slow."

"It was awful nice of you to come here and check on this problem, even though it wasn't real."

"That's our job, ma'am."

"Would you boys like a nice, tall, cold glass of iced tea? I've made fresh just a few minutes ago."

"We sure would, ma'am, but we can't. We've got to answer another call. It was real nice of you to offer," said the burley man as he turned to leave.

"Thank you," mumbled his skinny compadre.

I watched the men climb into their truck, use the radio to communicate with their dispatcher, and drive off slowly without a care in the world.

"Nikki, old girl, I believe we now know more than we did. But what we're going to do with the information, I haven't a clue."

I crossed the street and heard the faint sound of a ringing telephone. I took off running as fast as these fat little feet could carry me and reached the telephone after it had sounded off several times.

"Hello," I panted into the receiver.

"Ellen, are you all right?"

"Sure, I was running to get to the phone. I was outside with Nikki. What do you need, Barry?"

"I wanted to check on you. You seem to need my help on occasion. Is everything all right? You haven't called. I was worried about you."

"I'm not a wimp, Barry. I took care of myself long before you came into the picture," I answered a little too short.

"I didn't mean anything was wrong with you needing me, Ellen. As a matter of fact, I liked the idea that you might need me."

I wanted to bite my lip and take back my ugly words, but it was too late.

"I didn't mean anything bad either, Barry. It's just been a rough couple of days. Have you found out anything new about Eddy, Maggie, and Marty?"

"No. It's like they just fell off the face of the Earth. Nobody knows nothing, or if they do, they aren't talking. We have shaken a lot of different trees but haven't gotten even a hint of a lead. I want to ask you a few questions about the FBI agents you've talked with. Maybe they are not what they seem to be."

"My thoughts exactly. They seem to show up when you least expect them with the flimsiest excuses for being there."

"Have you talked to them again?"

"Yes."

"When?"

"Yesterday."

"What did they want?"

"They were trying to pump me for any information I might have about the little white house across the street."

"Did they have any luck?"

"What do you think?"

"I think you did everything but answer any direct questions. Am I right?"

"You sure are."

"What did they say?"

"They were trying to convince me that they were looking for bank robbers whom they thought might be hiding in that house, from what I deduced from their vague explanations."

"Did you believe what they said?"

"Not one word."

"You know they aren't required to tell you the truth. The law actually says they can lie to you. But, if you lie to them, you're in a lot of hot water. You didn't lie, did you?"

"No, not really. I didn't know anything for sure about that little white house. All I can do is guess. So, that's not lying, not in my book anyway."

"Good. I'm glad you didn't do or say anything weird, if you know what I mean. What did these guys look like? Did they give you their names?"

"Sure, Agent Thompson and Agent Chandler. Thompson is the one who usually does the talking. Appears to me that Chandler has been told to sit this one out as far as speaking is concerned."

"What did they look like?"

"Like feds with the gray suit, conservative tie, and nondescript car that would blend in my neighborhood without question."

"What about their hair?"

"What about it?"

"What was the color?"

"Brown, both had brown hair."

"How was it cut?"

"Thompson's was trimmed properly above the collar but Agent Chandler's was a little longer, more over his collar."

"They didn't tell you they were undercover, did they?"

"No."

"This Agent Chandler, was there anything different about him in particular?"

"Yeah, I told you he didn't talk."

"Do you think he has the ability to talk? Maybe he's a mute?"

"Would the FBI hire a mute?"

"You have a good point there. What do you think he was doing?"

"I think he was taking everything in, observing you might say, like he was Agent Thompson's supervisor or something like that."

"I've found out something that I need to tell you about, but I want to explain it to you face to face. Do you want me to come down to the police station? Or, would that be too much of a bother?"

"No, Ellen, you aren't a bother. Why don't I stop by your place on my way home? Have you eaten yet?"

"No, I haven't."

"I'll stop at the Chicken Hut and grab a bucket of chicken. Is that okay with you?"

"Sounds great. About what time?"

"How about now?"

"I can't wait." I whispered excitedly in the telephone.

I hung up the telephone and smiled. I really wanted to see Barry. I wanted him to hold me and tell me that he would make all of my problems go away forever. Was I falling in love with him? I didn't have any answer to that question of the heart, not yet anyway.

"Nikki, let's straighten up a little in this messy old place. We are going to have company and you're going to get some chicken for supper."

CHAPTER 15: FOUR PEOPLE MISSING

I knew about how long it should take to drive from the police station to my house and that was no longer than ten minutes, tops.

"Maybe the Chicken Hut was busy, Nikki. We'll give him a few more minutes before we get worried," I said as I stroked Nikki's tiny head.

I paced the floor, peeking out the window every few seconds, as I watched for his car to pull up and park in my driveway. I heard the sounds of a car and, upon inspection from my front window, I discovered that it was not Barry's car driving along the road, but I could see a car almost out of sight parked against the curb. From the part of the fender of the vehicle that I could glimpse, the color was the same as Barry's car.

"Why would Barry park over there? He should have pulled directly into my driveway. How long has he been there? I haven't heard the sounds of any cars passing the house except the one that this minute drove by and it wasn't him. Let's go check this out, Nikki." I said as I grabbed Nikki from the floor and raced to my back door. I grabbed my house key and shoved it in my pocket,

173

I didn't want anyone going into my house, again, without my invitation.

I closed my door quietly listening for the lock to snap into place. When I turned to walk down the steps I had to fight off a cold chill that had penetrated my heart.

I tried to sneak around my house but I knew I had to look pretty stupid. There was no way a woman of my bulk could sneak anywhere. That's not to say that I was anywhere near grotesque, just that crouching low to the ground and hiding behind a bush or a tree would have been difficult.

"Nikki, we've got to let it all hang out. There's no way I can make myself shrink to pencil size and hide behind the trees," I said as I tried to hide my fear from myself and my dog.

Nikki's eyes were wide taking in all of her surroundings and her tiny body was as taut as a spring that had been wound to breaking point.

"It is Barry's car, Nikki, but he's not in it. At least, I don't see him yet. Maybe he's slumped over in the front seat. Maybe he's had a heart attack. Oh God, I hope I'm wrong," I cried as I hurried as fast as I could to reach the car.

"It's empty, Nikki. No, not quite empty, the bucket of chicken is sitting on the back seat. Should I be grateful that he's not in it? Should I be worried that he's not in it? Well, the answer to that seems obvious to me. What do you think?"

Nikki's response was a whimper and slight movement of her tail.

What had happened to Barry? Why wasn't he in his car? Why wasn't he knocking at my door with the bucket of chicken under his arm? Why do all of the people I know and love disappear?

I had a bright idea. I was going to use Nikki as a tracking dog. Well, maybe it wasn't so bright after all. When I placed her on the pavement around Barry's car she merely cringed in fear. I wondered if she knew something that I didn't know. If only she could talk. What a help that would be, not to mention that fact that she would be a lot of company to this lonely old lady. I snatched her back up from the pavement. I certainly didn't want her to disappear.

I walked back to the house and called the police station.

"Barry Johnson is missing."

"Who is Barry Johnson?" asked the soft spoken man that had answered the insistent ringing of at least ten times.

"Your Barry Johnson, he's a cop."

"What do you mean 'he's missing'?"

"His car is parked near my house. Well, it's one house over from me. He was on his way to my house with a bucket of chicken for us to eat together and he never made it here. The chicken is in plain sight on the back seat of his car but he is gone, totally gone," I could hear the pitch of my voice getting higher and higher as the reality of the situation hit me.

"Who are you?"

"I'm Ellen Holcombe."

"You're the lady he has been trying to help find someone, aren't you?"

"Yes, counting Barry, I have four people missing from my life."

"I'll send someone to your house. What's your address?"

"I don't know if anyone should come here," I cried in the telephone.

"Why ma'am?"

"Whoever comes here will probably disappear, too!" I blubbered.

I couldn't talk anymore. The tears of frustration and fear that had built up so much pressure inside of me finally broke loose and sobs racked my entire being to the point that I could do nothing else but cry.

Nikki never left my side. She tried to console me by pawing gently at my hands that were covering my face and licking any exposed part of my skin with her tongue but nothing would work. I was inconsolable and scared to death.

Would I be next? Why hadn't I been the one they had taken in the first place? What in God's name was happening to everyone who knows me? Why? Why? Why? Why? Why?

There was a loud knock on my front door. It startled me for a moment. My heart raced with happiness with the thought that it was Barry. When I looked out the front window, I saw a uniformed cop poised and ready to knock again. I pecked on my window and pointed to the side of the house. I raced to the back door, down the steps, and to the corner of the house with Nikki following closely at my heels before he had a chance to get there.

"Officer, I'm Ellen Holcombe. Barry's car is parked right over there," I said as I pointed to the vehicle positioned in front of Maggie's house.

"Do you want to come with me while I check out the car?"

"Yes, please, if you don't mind. I don't want to get in the way."

"No problem, Mrs. Holcombe. Barry spoke very highly of you. I'm sure he wouldn't mind if you helped me a little," said the officer as a nice smile caused the corners of his mouth to turn up.

We walked together in silence after I bent over to pick up Nikki. I didn't want her to run out into the road. It was much too dangerous with passing cars and all that could happen to the tiny little creature.

"Well, Mrs. Holcombe, you were right. The chicken is on the back seat. Do you happen to have a key to Barry's car?"

"Call me Ellen. No, I don't have a key."

"I'm going to my vehicle and get the tool I need to pop open his door. You wait right here, if you don't mind."

"Sure, no problem."

I watched him walk to his car. His backside, his walking gait, reminded me of the police officer that had entered the little white house across the street a few days earlier.

I watched as he pulled the tool from the trunk of his car. Then he walked to the front of his car, reached inside and pulled up a pair of rubber gloves. Before walking toward Barry's car, he spoke into the small radio receiver that was attached to the shoulder of his uniform telling the dispatcher where he was and what he was planning to do.

"Send back-up," was the phrase that came to me loud and clear.

Had he seen something that I hadn't seen? If so, what was it?

"Mrs. Holcombe, we need to go back to your house."

"Why?"

"I need to ask you a few questions."

I looked at him like he was speaking a foreign language. Ask me a few questions? Why? I'm not the person who is missing. Barry is.

Finally I closed my mouth and said, "Sure, follow me. We have to go around back. I had to nail the front door shut. You will probably find the reason for that in Barry's file. I reported it, you know."

"What did you report?"

"That someone had broken into my house."

"That's no reason to nail your door."

"It is when the thief removed the lock by cutting it out and ruining the door for good. I have to buy a new door because of that cute trick," I said with the bitterness corroding my words.

"What was taken?"

"I don't have a clue. I couldn't find anything missing. I thought maybe whoever did the cutting was trying to put something into my house."

"Like what, Mrs. Holcombe?"

I was getting flustered with these questions about me and not about Barry.

"Maybe the person was planting a bug, a bomb, a piece of evidence, I don't know what that person did or why?"

"Why would anybody want to do that?"

"Don't you cops talk to each other? You know Barry is trying to locate my best friend Maggie who went missing first. Then my son Eddy vanished. Marty, Maggie's son is gone. Now, Barry is missing. Officer, these are all people I know and love. Barry was trying to help me find them," I said in a tone that was near screaming.

"Calm down, Mrs. Holcombe. Tell me about your friend Maggie."

"Read the damn file, Officer. What's your name? Officer who?"

"Roy Anderson is my name and I will read the file, but for now, you're the only person who knows anything about what's going on."

"I'm sorry, Roy, I don't know what to think about everybody disappearing. You had better watch your step. You might be next."

"Yes ma'am. Now, about Maggie, then Eddy, next is Marty, and last is Barry. Start talking so we can have an idea of what to do next."

"What about your back-up? Should I wait until they get here?"

"No, I will have them investigate around Barry's car."

"Did you see something odd in or around Barry's car?"

179

"Just some scuffles in the dirt on the driver side. Some heel scuffs and drag marks were there."

"Are you sure? I didn't see any of those marks."

"I'm not really sure, no. That is why I called for back-up. I want another trained eye to take a look see."

"What can I do to help?"

"Just tell me everything you know. Please don't leave anything out," he demanded.

CHAPTER 16: RISING HOPE

I explained to Officer Roy Anderson everything I could remember about my loved ones vanishing from my world. He looked a little skeptical. What could I say? I didn't blame him for the skepticism.

When they finally decided to depart from the scene, I was relieved to have the accusatory looks from the investigators gone from within my line of vision. They didn't take Barry's car, not yet anyway. They decided to let it sit right where it was just in case he came back.

They dusted my front door for fingerprints, checked my telephone lines for bugs, and looked for bombs or incendiary devices that could burst into flame. There were four of them poking, prodding, and searching. Oddly enough, one of the cops was a lady with dark brown hair and nervous eyes. They told me nothing was found except a few fingerprints on the front door that most likely were either mine or Barry's. I didn't have much hope after they left so Nikki and I locked ourselves in for the night and went to bed to try to get some rest because I was going to start a new search as soon as the sun rose to chase the night away.

I had made no mention of the little white house across the street. Nor were there any questions asked of me regarding that house. I found that strange because the inhabitants would be neighbors of mine, if there were any inhabitants, that is.

With the rising sun, came rising hope. I was going to go to the library.

With the help of my coworker, Sylvia, I had been permitted to take a few days of vacation to try to handle my personal problems. Sylvia had promised to cover for me the best she could in my absence which then would allow me the freedom to stick my nose into everything that affected me in all aspects of my life. I didn't have very many days of freedom left to spend on my so-called personal problems. Of course, those who had labeled my problems as personal had no idea that those problems basically were a matter of life or death for the missing people and for me who might become the next missing person. It's only logical to think that that might happen. If they had known the truth, I'm sure I wouldn't have been so rushed to find some answers. I didn't want to tell them the truth, I was afraid anyone to whom I mentioned the disappearances might also vanish from my life.

Since I wasn't at work sitting in front of my computer, I had to locate another way to surf the Internet. I had no computer at home, for which I will be eternally sorry. So the next best thing was to use the computers marked for public use at the local library. I was most thankful that our small Stillwell County Libraries, all three of them, had computers for the public that were Internet accessible. In an area that was slow to accept computers, the school system and the libraries forged ahead leading the counties' children to a sparkling future.

"May I help you?"

"Yes ma'am, I need to do some research on the computer."

"I need your library card. Have you signed up for Internet usage?"

"No, I've never used the computer here before today. What do I need to do?"

"Let me have your card. I will sign you up for the Internet. You need to sign this card after which I will swipe it through our system and you can surf all you want. Follow me and I'll get you started."

"Thank you so much. I had no idea it was this easy."

"Have you used the Internet before?"

"Yes ma'am, I use it at work but I've taken a few days of vacation and I don't want to show up at the office just to use the Internet. I don't think that would be too cool, do you?"

"No, I guess not," she said with a smile.

I sat before the eye into the world of technology and thought about all of the tidbits of information that were stored in the maze of knowledge. How was I going to find out anything that I could use to help me find my family and friends? How was I going to protect myself from the same fate that had befallen them? What was the fate that had befallen them?

The bank robbery or armored truck robbery, whatever it was, seemed to be filtering into my pursuit of my missing loved ones.

I entered "bank robbery" and "Virginia" into the brain of the computer and pressed "search".

Boy, was I surprised to find out how many bank robberies that had taken place in the state of Virginia.

Well, I needed to narrow the search so I added the word "Bluefield".

That was better, that gave me about half as many references. I knew I didn't have the time to check them all so I decided to try "armored truck robbery" and "Bluefield".

"Bingo!"

There were only about five reference points so I started reading.

I was looking for a date about two months earlier.

I found it and it even supplied photographs. They were good photos when you consider that they consisted of the grainy texture of surveillance tape. How they ever made it onto the Internet was beyond me. It was hard to distinguish, but the two faces that were captured on the film looked vaguely familiar.

The article mentioned the possibility of the robbery having been planned as an inside job. It referred to one of the perpetrators as being a current employee, a security guard, who was aided in the robbery by a former employee. Both men were under investigation but that was all.

Under investigation meant that they were sure they didn't have enough evidence to convict.

My mind and eyes went back to the grainy photograph. There was something about the picture that was trying to make itself known.

I asked for help to get a print of the article and the black and white photographs. After paying for my five sheets of paper, I stuffed them into my handbag for safekeeping.

Now, on to the next topic.

I entered "Jonathan Smith Alexandria VA" and received notification of results of forty six thousand four hundred possibilities.

"Jeez," I mumbled as I thought the whole world was named Jonathan Smith from Alexandria, Virginia. Of course, I forgot that the computer picked out all references with any of the four words.

Next, I keyed in "Jonathan Smith Stillwell" and received a much smaller slate of results to the tune of four thousand four hundred fifty.

I decided to use the address of 302 Valleyview Street and was shown only seven hundred thirty four results. That was a much more reasonable response, but it was based on an address that Jonathan Smith had never used for himself to my knowledge and understanding.

I had noticed on the search page the listing of companies who find people for you through their web site at a cost. It does allow you to see the name listing free of charge. I entered Jonathan Smith in Alexandria VA and fourteen matches were displayed. If I wanted to see any specific details as related to the displayed matches, I would have to pay for the privilege.

Since the initial search was free, I entered "Jonathan Smith VA" to see what would be shown on the screen. I received one hundred results from every corner of the state. I was shown another one hundred results when I entered "Jonathan Smith" without reference to any state.

185

The state locations ranged from AK-Alaska to AR-Arkansas that told me that there were many more that I had not received.

When I selected a different search company, I received some overlapping responses to what I had already chosen.

I printed the people search information for Jonathan Smith of Alexandria VA and the 302 Valleyview Street information for my records at a cost of twenty-five cents per page and concluded my Internet session for the time being.

After I uncover some more specific information, I would search again.

For now, I needed to go rescue Nikki from the car and make my way to the post office.

"Hi, I'm Ellen Holcombe and I live at 305 Valleyview Street. I wonder if you might be able to help me. I am looking for the name of the person who lives at 302 Valleyview Street so I can report that I saw someone going through the mailbox. I just want to make sure that I'm not reporting the person who really should be receiving the mail."

"I'm sorry, ma'am, we aren't allowed to give out that information."

"Well, okay, can you tell me if you have a person's name listed as receiving mail at that location?"

"At this time, the mail is being forwarded to another address."

"Does Mr. Jonathan Smith plan to move here?"

"There is no indication of that."

"The forwarding address in Alexandria, could you tell me the street number please?"

"I'm sorry; I'm not at liberty to say."

"You know I'm only trying to help. I'm quite sure Jonathan Smith was not the one searching the mailbox because he's still in Alexandria."

"I'm sorry, ma'am. Mr. Smith would have to report the problem with the mail or the postal inspector would have to catch the thief in the act. There's not much more that I can do."

"That's all right. Maybe it's best that I stay out of this entirely, if you know what I mean. Thanks for your help," I said as I cheerfully walked out of the post office.

That poor postal clerk had no idea that she had answered every one of my questions without any direct statements.

I was being underhanded in a sneaky way in trying to obtain all of the information I could about the little white house across the street. How was I going to prove it? How was I going to find out who was living there? Why were there no signs of persons, at least four according to the water company, turning on and off the lights, entering and exiting, opening and closing the blinds or shades or even the drapes?

Who mowed the grass? Once I found out who the mower was, I could probably find out how that person got paid.

Was there a telephone? A phone bill, maybe there was a phone bill that was being forwarded to Mr. Jonathan Smith in Alexandria, Virginia. Maybe, just maybe, I could get the phone company to mail a duplicate phone bill at the address of the location of the telephone, meaning the little white house, of course, because Jonathan Smith's copy had been thrown out with the garbage in error. I was his secretary, Mary Jameson, and I was making this call at his request because he was out of the country for a couple of weeks.

"Nikki, do you think that will work? I hope so. Let's go find that pay phone again."

I dropped the change into the pay phone and called the telephone company after I looked up the number in the battered book that was hanging from a chain.

"Hello, my name in Mary Jameson and I need to get a copy of a phone bill for my boss. I think I threw it away by accident and he's really going to get mad at me if I don't pay the bill while he's away on business."

"Is this for a residence or a business?"

"A residence."

"What's the telephone number you are calling about with the area code first?"

"I can tell you the area code and the first three numbers of the seven digit listing. I can't remember what the other four numbers are and I didn't write it down anywhere. Mr. Smith usually takes care of this but like I said, he's away on business."

"What is the name again?"

"His name is Jonathan Smith and the location of the line is at 302 Valleyview Street."

"One moment please. Yes, I have it here. It will take a few days to process this request."

"Don't mail it to the address in Alexandria, Virginia; instead, mail it to the house where the phone line is located. He will be visiting in a couple of weeks and I want to make sure the bill gets paid. I will be at that location in a couple of days getting it ready for his arrival. Would it be a problem to change the address?"

"No, ma'am. Is that where you want us to mail any future bills?"

"Yes, please, that would be nice."

"Is there anything else, ma'am?"

"How many days do you think it will take?"

"I'll put a rush on it and maybe you'll get it in a couple of days."

"Thank you so much," I gushed trying to sound like a relieved employee who was trying to cover up her major blunder.

I smiled as I walked back to the car with Nikki cradled in my arms.

"Doesn't take much to pick up my spirits just a little bit," I said into the backside of my precious pet as I nuzzled her slightly with my nose.

CHAPTER 17: BIGGEST GOSSIP IN TOWN

I passed the mail carrier as I was driving to the house. I put my thoughts into gear and decided it was high time I stood by my mailbox and passed the time of day with Shirley Ayers, our rural route postal worker and biggest gossip in town, or so I had been told.

I needed a reason to be lurking outside awaiting Shirley's arrival at my mailbox, so I quickly wrote out a check to pay a bill that was almost past due. I didn't attach a stamp to it because that was going to be my reason for standing by the mailbox. I needed a stamp to mail my bill payment.

I stood on my front porch and watched Shirley stop at every mailbox on the street and talk to every passerby she could find. It was no wonder that Shirley was a gossip. She knew everybody and if she didn't know them she would talk to them anyway.

Finally, the giant box shaped vehicle rolled up to my mailbox.

"Shirley, how are you?" I asked in a neighborly tone.

"Fine, Ellen, fine. I hope everything is good with you and yours."

"Good, good, couldn't be better," I lied brazenly.

"What are you doing home from work? Taking a vacation day?"

"As a matter of fact I am but I discovered that I forgot to mail this bill and it's almost late. If I was at work I would pay it over the Internet, but since I don't have a computer at home, I have to use your services. Come to think of it, I bet the Internet sure cuts into your business at the post office, doesn't it?"

"Yes, Ellen, it surely does. What is it that I can help you with?"

"I need a stamp, if you don't mind?"

"Will one be enough?"

"No, you better give me a book of stamps; I plan to do some letter writing. Letter writing has become a lost art, you know."

"Yeah, I know what you mean, I work for the post office and I don't like to write letters. Seems a little silly, doesn't it?"

"Speaking of letters, you see that house across the street?"

"Yeah, the one with its back to the road?"

"Yes, that's the one. The people that were living there moved out. Did they leave a forwarding address?"

"You mean the Browns, the middle-aged couple?"

"Yes. I have received delivery of something that I can't return that belongs to them. I need to know where to send it. I need to make sure that they get it."

"You can take it to Detective Green at the police station. He is the one who gets their mail and forwards it to the Browns. I don't know the reason for the secrecy, but Detective Green can help you get the stuff to the Browns."

"What about Mr. Smith, the guy who owns the place? I have a letter in the house that came to me and it should have gone to him. I know he gets his mail in Alexandria but I don't have the street address. Can you get that for me? I will put his mail in another envelope and mail it to him myself with a little note of explanation."

"I might be able to give you that right now. Let me see," Shirley said as she fanned through some envelopes that had been tossed to the side. "Here it is. It's a letter I must have tossed in the wrong bin when I was sorting the route mail this morning. That happens, you know. We all can't be perfect like some I know who claim to be."

"Can you wait here a minute, I need a piece of paper to write this address down."

"Wait a second, Ellen. I'll pull this sticker off of the envelope. It'll peel right up. I'll put another one on it when I get back to the post office."

"Are you sure? You won't get into trouble, will you?"

"No problem. Who is going to know it just didn't fall off of the envelope. I told you, they just peel up. Sometimes that's a good thing, like now. Most of the time it's a pain."

"Thank you so much, Shirley. This really helps. I don't know if the letter is important or not but I don't feel right holding on to it for so long."

"No problem, Ellen."

"Oh, Shirley, I saw some furniture being moved into the place the other day. Do you know who will be living there now?"

"No, there hasn't been anything filed at the post office and no new names have appeared on the mail for that address. Have you seen any one there?"

"No, just the moving van people. At least, I think it was the moving van people."

"What do you mean by that? Why wouldn't it be moving van people?"

"The men were too manicured and tailored, if you know what I mean."

"Who or what do you think they were?" Shirley's curiosity was reaching its peak.

"Undercover cops or secret agents maybe?"

"For real? You think they were real secret agents? What kind of secret agents?"

"I don't have a clue. It makes sense though, you know."

"How's that?"

"You said the mail was being forwarded to that Detective Green. Wouldn't it be possible that the people who move in and out of this house might be hiding from someone or something with the help of the cops?"

"Are you making this up, Ellen? You being a writer and all? You aren't trying to pull my leg, are you?"

"I swear I'm not lying to you about this house in any way, shape or form, Shirley. I think it's dangerous for me to be living across the street from a house that could be hiding people, like drug dealers, organized crime bosses, or spies."

"I see your point, Ellen. It really could be dangerous."

"Shirley, do me a really big favor, okay?"

"That depends on the favor, Ellen. I can't promise you anything, especially if it's illegal."

"I wouldn't ask you to do anything illegal, Shirley. At least, I wouldn't do anything like that on purpose. All I would like is for you to keep your eyes and ears open for anything you might hear about that house and the people who own or live in it."

"Oh, sure, Ellen, no problem. I can do that without a doubt. How long are you going to be on vacation?"

"The next couple of weeks, I think. Had to use up some days before I lost them. You know how that is."

"Yeah, it really hurts to give days back to the company."

"So you don't mind keeping watch for me?"

"No problem. I'll drive by your place about the same time everyday delivering the mail. If you meet me at the mailbox, I'll tell you everything I've heard at that time. Is that okay?"

"That's great, Shirley."

"I'll see you tomorrow, Ellen."

CHAPTER 18: HELP ME. SYLVIA

"Now what, Nikki?"

Nikki isn't going to answer me. I know that. I'm not totally crazy, not yet anyway.

"I wonder why I haven't been snatched up like Eddy, Marty, and Maggie." I said as I continued talking to my only companion in life at this point in time. "Why have they left me wandering around the world asking questions, doing research, stirring up dust everywhere I go?

"Maggie was the first to go. Why Maggie and not me? Does Maggie have some kind of secret past? Is someone out there afraid of me? Why? Why would anyone be afraid of me? Who am I that I would earn such fear?

"Maybe I know someone that might put two and two together and come up with an answer. Who? I haven't led an unusual life. I was born into upper poverty level. Meaning my dad, every once in a while, could afford a frivolous item or two. Not often, mind you.

"Take Christmas, for example. I would get a doll every Christmas whether I wanted one or not. One Christmas I got a Toni doll which is a sought after collector's item nowadays and it had to cost a pretty penny back then.

195

Keep in mind I always got a doll and I didn't want a doll. I wanted games such as Monopoly and Scrabble that I could play in the company of other kids my age.

"Needless to say the doll was not my favorite. It didn't take me long to whack off its wiry red hair and make it even uglier than it was.

"Oh, Nikki, how did I get all the way to Christmas? Girl, I sure do wish you could talk. Oh well, it actually helps me to hear myself talk about my problems to you. You're such a good listener. Believe it or not, you are a big help."

I sat on the sofa and fell asleep as if I had not a care in the world. Nikki's gentle kindness and understanding as she snuggled herself in my arms served as a sedative. We were both seeking the same peaceful, restful sleep that innocence brings into your dreams.

That was not to be.

****

I saw the little white house across the street as it weaved and bobbed like some kind of dancing fool taunting and teasing me until I clenched my fists into white-knuckle hardness. I couldn't take a swing at a house, or could I? I was dreaming, wasn't I? You can do all kinds of impossible things in dreams.

I reached up and tried to punch the house. If I hit it hard enough, would all of the air rush out of it like a deflating balloon? That was my theory. I swung again and again trying to pop that balloon. The house was dancing barely out of my reach bobbing and weaving faster than ever until abruptly all movement stopped including my swinging arms that had dropped to my sides and were parallel to my body on the bed.

196

My sleeping eyes wandered over the face, that's what it was, a leering face, as it stood perfectly still allowing me to see inside the very limited space provided by an unfettered window into the nightmarish world of the little white house across the street.

Maggie's face appeared at the window. It was not the pleasant face of my dear friend but it was an image of Maggie purpled and distorted from lack of oxygen because of the knotted noose hanging down the front of her blouse making it appear that she had been cut loose from a rope that had been thrown over a rafter or tree limb. Her head was tilted to the side as if her neck were broken. Her mouth was hanging open in a permanent scream and her eyes were wide in terror.

I moaned as I fought the image. I tried to push it away. I didn't believe what I was seeing. I couldn't believe what I was seeing.

Suddenly Maggie disappeared and Marty was shoved forward to the window where I could see that he was displaying a trickle of blood from every body orifice that the window allowed me to see. His mouth was clenched and his eyes were closed tightly but the blood continued to trickle. A stick of some sort appeared and shoved Marty slightly forcing his head to turn from one side to the other so I could see the blood trickling from each of his ears.

Marty looked like he was still alive, just barely.

Marty was moved to the side allowing the appearance of Barry to fill the window.

I sucked in a deep breath when I saw Barry's badge that had been pinned to the bare skin of his chest. Barry's head was pitched forward and his mouth was moving in what looked to be prayer.

"Oh, God, Barry, what have I done to you?" I cried as the scene changed again.

"Eddy, Eddy, is that you?" I sputtered when I saw my son's long dark brown hair fly out away from his head making it look as if someone had slapped Eddy wickedly hard on his back.

Eddy tried to focus his eyes as if he were looking for me.

"I'm here, baby, I'm here. Where are you? I can't find you. Give me a sign. Let me know so I can come get you."

I saw Eddy's mouth move like he was trying to speak. I couldn't hear him nor could I read his lips.

"Eddy, louder, speak louder, please."

His lips formed words and then he was gone.

The drapes at the window started to close signaling that my foray into the nightmarish world of the vile white house across the street had come to an end.

I opened my eyes, blinked rapidly, and climbed from my bed.

It was only a dream.

****

"This is Ellen Holcombe. Have you made any progress on locating Barry Johnson, Martin Boothe, Eddy Holcombe, and Maggie Boothe?" I said slowly into the telephone.

"Mrs. Holcombe, you need to speak with Detective Green. He has a few questions to ask you."

"Yeah, sure, when?"

"Can you come to the station now?"

"Yeah, okay, I'll have to get dressed. It'll probably be about an hour."

"Detective Green will be expecting you."

I didn't like the sound of that. What were they thinking? Maybe they think I had something to do with the disappearances?

Well, I guessed I did. It's just that I didn't know what involvement I did have.

What if they gave me a lie detector test? Because of the way I felt, I was sure I would have a reaction that would indicate to them that I had something to do with this whole mess.

What if they locked me up?

Why was I still free?

I couldn't go to the police station. Nikki and I had some more investigating to do. I couldn't do it from a jail cell.

I hurriedly dressed, let myself out of my back door, and ran to my car with Nikki clutched securely against my body.

Not more than twenty minutes had passed after my conversation with the officer. It appeared that an hour was too long for Detective Green to wait for me to present myself for interrogation at the police station. As I drove my car in the opposite direction I caught sight of flashing blue lights with the added attraction of screaming sirens as a police vehicle stopped abruptly in front of the house I had just left.

"Oh, my God," I mumbled as I stepped on the gas pedal to propel myself away from the scene. "Nikki, what are we going to do?" I cried as I fought to keep my car on the road. The tears of fear and frustration were blinding me but I knew I couldn't pull over to the side of the road because I was too close to home.

I drove.

I had no destination in mind. Nikki and I were on our own. I had only the clothes on my back and whatever amount of money there was in my wallet. I wasn't even sure how much money that was.

"I'm going to try to find Sylvia, Nikki. Maybe she can help me. After all, we work together and she is my friend. She's not my best friend. That's reserved for Maggie and Maggie alone."

I drove to the next small town to locate a pay phone. Why didn't I ever get a cell phone? Oh yeah, they probably could have traced the call. The disposable cells would do the trick. I'll have to get one of those.

"Sylvia Matthews, please." I said into the telephone receiver in a tone of voice much lower pitched than my normal tone.

"May I say who is calling?" asked the high school student who was working in the office part-time as part of her school assignment.

"Linda Hutchins, I used to work with Sylvia." It wasn't a complete lie. Linda was my middle name and Hutchins was my maiden name."

"Hello, this is Sylvia."

"This is Ellen. Please don't say my name out loud. I don't think you'll want anyone to know that you're talking to me," I said in an excited whisper.

"Okay, Linda was it? What can I do for you?"

"Help me, Sylvia. Please help me. I don't know what to do next. I'm afraid to talk to anybody face to face. I'm afraid if whoever is doing this to me finds out about you, you'll be next."

"Why? What are you talking about?"

"Has anybody been to the office questioning you guys about me?"

"Not that I know of. Why would that happen?"

"Sylvia, there are people missing from my life. Barry Johnson is the cop trying to help me find my son, Eddy, and now they are both gone. It started when I found that my neighbor, Maggie, was missing and now her son, Marty, is gone, too."

"I don't understand," whispered Sylvia. She must have cupped her hand around the receiver to hide her conversation from anyone who might be close by.

"Neither do I, Sylvia. Now the police think I have something to do with the disappearances. I swear to you that I don't, Sylvia. I don't have any idea why they are gone."

"What do you want me to do?"

"I need a different car. Do you have one I could borrow for a couple of days? I won't be leaving the county or anything like that, I promise. I'm sure the cops will be looking for my car. You can lock it up in your garage as collateral if you like."

"I don't know if I should get involved."

"Please, Sylvia, I don't know who else to ask," I pleaded with all of the sincerity I could muster.

"Let me think about it. Is there anything else?"

"Money, all I have is what is in my handbag and that isn't much. I wasn't expecting to be hiding from the cops, if you know what I mean. I'll write you a check for a couple hundred dollars and you can hold it until this blows over or I get arrested, whichever comes first. If anyone asks, it's a loan repayment from way back."

"I'll have to go to the bank."

"I know."

"Call me back in a couple of hours."

"Sure, Sylvia, and thanks."

"I haven't done anything yet."

"Yes you have. You've given me hope. I need that more than anything. There's just one more thing, Sylvia."

"What's that?"

"Don't tell the cops that we have talked."

Apprehension crawled up my spine when I placed the receiver back into its cradle. Had I made a mistake by calling Sylvia? After all, we were only coworkers, not real friends. The only thing the two of us had in common was work. Was that enough of a foundation to ask her for what more than likely would be illegal help?

I walked back to the car and sat with Nikki while I watched people enter and leave the convenience store in whose parking lot I was hiding in plain sight. The lot circled around the store allowing me to park away from the main road.

I was watching the people, trying to see if I recognized anyone. If I was able to recognize them, I was sure they would recognize me, and I didn't want that to happen.

"Wait here, Nikki. I need some coffee and something to eat. I'll get you a sausage biscuit and some water. I know you're hungry," I said as I locked the car door while Nikki's pleading eyes followed my every movement.

I never knew how hard it was to be inconspicuous without looking obvious about the fact that you were hiding from someone.

The inability to look someone straight in the eye was a dead giveaway. I entered the store slowly and looked around the place quickly turning my head from side to side as I searched for bodies and cameras. The bodies represented possible recognition. The cameras were a permanent recording of my presence meaning that I was no longer hidden.

The place was empty except for the clerk who was standing behind the counter watching me.

"May I help you with something?" she asked in a lilting tone.

"Yes, I need some coffee. Do you have any breakfast sandwiches left?" I answered with a fake smile forcing the corners of my mouth up in clown like fashion.

"Coffee is over there. We have several kinds of biscuit sandwiches. What would you like?'

"One sausage, it's not hot sausage is it?" I asked as I placed the plastic lid onto the large cup of black coffee.

"No, just regular breakfast sausage. I don't sell the hot stuff. My customers don't like that for breakfast. Anything else?"

"Yes, one biscuit with sausage, egg, and cheese. You better make it two. I'm really hungry. Oh, I almost forgot,

I need a bottle of water," I said as I started digging around inside my handbag for money.

"The water is in the cooler in the back. I'll ring everything up after you get your water."

I walked to the back of the store and heard the door open in the front while I was hidden from view. When I looked up I was shocked to see a State Trooper standing at the counter. I ducked my head, hiding my presence from the State Trooper.

I strained my ears as I tried to zero in on any conversation that might be passing between the State trooper and the clerk.

I heard the sound of the front door again and then I looked around the grocery aisle to check out the reason for the sound, I noticed the clerk was alone again.

"You hiding from the cops?" asked the curious store clerk.

"Why would you ask that?" I sputtered.

"You hid while the State Trooper was in here."

"It's nothing really. Just a misunderstanding but I'm not ready to explain it. I still have some digging to do. You know ex-husbands and all that," I lied as I tried to make my problem sound domestic.

"Is the trooper your ex?"

"Not exactly. He's a friend of my ex."

"Oh, I see," said the confused clerk.

"How much do I owe you? I need to get to work," I continued to lie except this time the words came a lot easier.

I gathered up my purchases and exited the store slowly so as not to cause the store clerk any more concern. I thought a fast exit might implant my visit permanently in her memory. Even though I was pretty sure it would take a long time for her to forget me after my obvious avoidance of the cop.

I walked to the car and settled in so I could drive away from the store. I needed to find a place where Nikki and I could eat in peace and then settle down for a rest.

I was so tired.

CHAPTER 19: A SCARY RIDE

I drove until I found a country road that led to a clearing where there were picnic tables and solitude. I could hear birds singing and the wind rustling through the trees but nothing else. There was absolutely no sound of human life anywhere around.

I have never felt more alone in my life. Even when my husband died, at least, there was family. I don't have a lot of family, but my work life and the members of that part of my world came to give me support.

My husband had been my life. I gave up all connections with the outside world when I married him. I was one of those people who ignored the girlfriends I had grown up with before my marriage until they were no longer any part of my life. I had not gone out of my way since my husband's death to find another person with whom I could share my world with other than Barry. I miss Barry. I was just getting to know him and to like him.

Of course, my boys were a big part of my life but they were no longer at home and part of my day to day existence. One son lived so very far away while the other son was missing.

My God, what was I supposed to do?

Maggie was the only friendship outside the family I had nurtured and I wanted that to remain in existence until death do us part. Maggie and I needed each other if only to hear each other bitch about how the world was treating us.

Nikki was my only companion now. What would I do without my little dog? I had to have some kind of foothold into my world of reality. She was the only thing keeping me on a steady keel at this point. She is a living and breathing part of the real world. Regardless of what had been going on around me, I could touch and hold Nikki and know that I was still hanging in there.

I knew I sounded stupid talking to my dog all the time, but what choice do I have? The sound of words after they have left my mouth was what helped me figure out what my next step would be. I would talk to Maggie much the same way I talked to my Nikki with the exception that Maggie could talk back to me and Nikki just looked at me with her huge round eyes. Hearing the words out loud was what set me on my course to good or evil.

"Nikki, we've got to get some answers. This depression is going to kill me if I keep wallowing in it for very long."

I started the car up, glanced at the gas gauge and saw that I didn't have much left in my tank. I took out my wallet and checked the cash. I only had about twenty dollars between me and poverty. I could always write a check. Hopefully, that wouldn't get me into hot water.

As I started to drive along the country road I caught a glimpse of another vehicle coming towards me. I didn't know whether to be happy or sad about the prospect of passing another human being along this isolated part of the county.

It didn't take me long to discover that the oncoming vehicle was one that I didn't want to see. The vehicle was moving slow — real slow — but it was still moving directly towards me. The blue lights were not flashing and the sirens were not blaring, but the passengers in the vehicle were staring straight at me. It's not that I could see their eyes because actually I wasn't close enough to see them, but I felt them searing into my skin.

Suddenly I said, "Take a picture, stupid. It will last longer," as I laughed hysterically at that silly, childish statement. I could remember saying those words to people who were staring at me when I was a child.

Nikki raised her front paws to the dashboard of the car in an effort to see out of the window.

"Get down, Nikki. I don't want you to get hurt."

Nikki whimpered and did as I told her.

I jabbed at the gas pedal with my foot. I caused the car to jump as I held out my hand to grab Nikki so she wouldn't mash her tiny body up against the dashboard. With the jumping motion of my car, the police vehicle swerved a bit to the opposite side of the road. That swerving motion gave me the room to get past the police car if I floored my gas pedal.

"Hang on, girl; we're in for a scary ride. Let's show the cops that this little old fat lady still has some moves left in her."

Nikki must have sensed a reason for fear because she jumped to the floor of my car and tried to crawl under the passenger seat.

I glanced at the rearview mirror and saw that the huge four wheel drive police vehicle was having a problem trying to make a u-turn on the narrow country road. Oh, there was space for the turn if you knocked down the corn crop that had been planted to the edge of the twelve inch width of gravel that extended beyond the pavement.

I knew the turning task had been completed when the sirens roared to life and I felt the police vehicle driving closer to me trying to close the gap I had caused with my little jumping action.

"Nikki, I'm adding speeding and whatever else they can think of to the charges they plan to throw at me. But – I can't let them catch me," I said as I sped onto the main road and headed toward town.

I glanced in my mirror again and I didn't see them so I pulled into the driveway of a farmhouse. It didn't look as if anyone was at home. I pulled around to the back of the house over the grass and as close to the house itself that I could get. I needed to hide, and this looked like the only place available. I was hoping the cops would think I was heading away from town and turn in the opposite direction when they came to the main road.

I waited with my head down and my body flat against the front seat. I reached my hand to the floor to comfort Nikki as much as I could without making a sound. She didn't bark, whine, or do anything that would draw attention to either of us. It was like the little critter could read my mind.

I could feel her tiny body shake from fear. My body was shaking a bit, too, except that my body was not quite so little.

I heard sirens but they were fading in the distance. They must have taken the wrong turn that was thankfully taking them away from town.

I sat up and breathed a sigh of relief.

"Let's go to town, Nikki. I've got a couple of things to do."

I was getting good at evading the law but that was not the type of thing I wanted to be good at, if you knew what I meant.

I had to find another telephone so I could call Sylvia. More than two hours had passed so I knew if Sylvia was going to help me, she had had plenty of time to gather up the items I asked for. "If" is a mighty big word when you think hard enough about what could happen if the "if" didn't come to pass.

If Sylvia didn't help me, what was I going to do next? How was I going to find my son and my friends?

CHAPTER 20: SAY WHAT, NIKKI?

"Sylvia, are you going to help me?" I whispered into the pay phone I had located at a gasoline station on the main road just outside of town.

"No, I can't. You shouldn't be calling me. The cops are crawling all over this place. What if they are recording this call," said a panicking Sylvia.

"If they are recording, Sylvia, then they know you've told me no. Thanks for nothing," I said as I angrily placed the receiver in its cradle.

I bought a cup of coffee from the machine just inside the office area and made my way back out to my car and to my little dog. At least, she would be glad to see me and hear my voice.

I cried and cried as I sat in my car stroking Nikki.

My world was caving in on me but I wasn't the only one with a problem. Maggie, Marty, Barry, and my son, Eddy, were in danger. I knew they were in danger and no one was doing anything to help them.

I really hadn't believed that Sylvia wouldn't help me. She was a friend, I thought, but people being the way they were, I was sure she didn't want to stick her neck out and get involved.

"Nikki, let's get Eddy's car. The cops won't be looking for it. They will be zeroed in on my car, but they, hopefully, haven't bothered to check on Eddy's."

I cruised into town abiding by all of the driving rules and regulations so that no one would notice me, a gray-haired old lady out for a drive in the late afternoon with her pet dog. This was one of the times I was grateful that I was a gray-haired, old lady because as such I didn't fit the profile of a wanted felon or serial killer.

Unlike most of my peers, I didn't mind the gray hair and the years. I wore my hair as a badge telling anyone interested that I was proud to be the age that I was and that I thanked God every day for my having made it this far. Of course, if anyone asked, I told them the old adage of "if I knew then what I know now" really applied because I was sure I would be a millionaire if I hadn't had to suffer through all the mistakes I encountered in my lifetime.

No one stopped me in town. "Whew, Nikki, we've made if this far."

I pulled into Eddy's driveway and exited the car so I could inspect the exterior of his house. I wanted to know if he had any telltale signs of unwanted visitors.

I carried Nikki in my arms as I strolled around the house trying not to look like a burglar. Nothing looked out of place so I climbed back into my car and pulled out a second set of keys. Eddy had a set of keys to my house and car and I had his just in case there was something wrong that prevented us from getting home to check on our belongings.

I took the keys and unlocked Eddy's driver side door. I climbed in and was relieved to see that he must have just filled his gas tank before parking his car because the gauge registered "full".

"Nikki, Eddy sure is a good kid," I said with a weepy sort of smile.

The darkness was beginning to creep in around the edges of my life. I think that was a good thing. It would make it more difficult for people to recognize me and that could be a great help because I was going to be snooping into and around areas that could be dangerous, especially for me.

I needed to drive by my house and check on things. I needed to know that what was mine still was mine.

I tucked my hair up under a baseball cap of Eddy's that I found in the car. I threw one of his jackets around my shoulders and slipped on a pair of tennis shoes that he had also left in the car. I was glad that we wore the same size shoe except that his shoe was man sized. My feet slid around a little inside the shoe but if I tied the laces really tight, I could wear them without a problem, I hoped.

I parked on the street a couple of houses away so no one would be sure where I was going. I held on to Nikki but kept her under my jacket so no one would know she was with me. All of my neighbors would know it was me because of Nikki if I allowed her to be seen.

I walked up to my front door and knocked. Sounded stupid didn't it? But I had to knock so that no one would know it was me. Then I walked to the back door and knocked again while I was unlocking the door. When I looked down at my feet I noticed the yellow police tape.

"Nikki, the cops have been here searching my house. They'll think I tore down the tape, but I didn't. You know I didn't. It was already torn down, wasn't it, girl?" I asked my dog wishing that she could testify for me when I was dragged into court for God knows what crimes.

I walked into the kitchen and took in the sight of total destruction, again. This was the second time my house had been turned upside down while it was being searched through every nook and cranny.

"Nikki, I don't think the cops did all of this. This kind of destruction shouldn't be allowed legally with a search warrant. There had to be another reason for this" I said as I kicked aside a pile of my clothes that had been clean and hanging in my closet prior to my departure to outrun the long arm of the law.

I locked my back door and ran upstairs to the bathroom where I was going to take a shower. A few broken bottles, not many because now most of the toiletries I purchased were in plastic containers. I was afraid to switch on a light. A well-meaning neighbor might call the cops.

I grabbed Nikki and we both jumped into the shower. It felt good to have the hot water running down my back and over all of the spots of my body that were absorbing tension and holding it until I felt like a coiled spring ready to let go.

Nikki didn't particularly like showers but she didn't mind it nearly as much if I were with her, holding her, and scrubbing her with baby shampoo. Talk about a drowned rat, poor thing. I shook my head and laughed at her as she tried to shake off what little water was left on her tiny body.

I heard a noise outside and realized that I had better get a move on. It was getting too dark to be walking around the house without any kind of light. I put on some clean clothes and grabbed a couple of changes to stash in the car. I grabbed Nikki's food and some bottled water along with her warm fuzzy blanket for the cool nights.

I ransacked the kitchen even more by kicking aside boxes and cans until I could find some food I could eat while living in Eddy's car. I remembered my money cache and hoped whoever had been searching the house had overlooked it.

I grabbed a book from the shelf in the dining room that had a hundred-dollar bill taped to the dustcover on the inside next to the bookbinding.

I peeked out a front window, then a side window, and finally the kitchen window before I attempted to open the back door. I didn't want to walk into any surprises. First, I deposited Nikki in the car so she would be safe. Then, I went back to get the supplies that I threw into the trunk of the car. I tried to make as little noise as possible. I didn't want the cops to come calling before I had a chance to do some more exploring.

It was dark enough so that I could walk across the street and check the mailbox for the little white house across the street without too much worry about being seen. Come to think of it, I didn't have any neighbors in the front of my house, so they tell me, because the little white house across the street was supposed to be empty of renters. Maggie was missing so that was another neighbor gone. The back of my house butted up against the railroad tracks that you had to cross before that neighbor whom I have never met could be seen. The only worrisome neighbor would be the one on the side where my back door was located. Fortunately, there were some tall shrubbery and a couple of small outbuildings that prevented the little old lady next door from keeping a constant vigil on my comings and goings. I guessed her age to be about eighty or eighty-five, but she had keen watchful eyes.

The mailbox I needed to rob was one of those new jobs that had a door in the front where the postal carrier loaded the box and a door in the rear for easy access by the owner. I started walking slowly on the sidewalk and stepped off onto the grass on the pretext of tying my shoe. While I was bent over I reached up my hand from the back of the box and grabbed the mail. I quickly shoved it into my jacket pocket, stood up from shoe tying, and walked back to the car. I started the car and drove away waving at a nonexistent person as I left the scene.

I drove around the block and parked a few spaces away from where I originally parked on the street. I grabbed a flashlight and began sorting through the mail that was mostly addressed to "occupant". It seemed they got a lot of the same junk mail that I got all of the time.

Once all the junk mail was eliminated, three business sized envelopes remained in my grasp.

I tore open the first envelope to discover a telephone bill that had been addressed to Jonathan Smith. Just as I had asked. The phone bill was mailed to 302 Valleyview Street instead of Alexandria, Virginia, where it had been previously addressed.

I memorized the telephone number that was written on the upper right hand corner of the billing statement and scrutinized the entire document looking for information that I could use. There had been some long

216

distance calls made to several different numbers. Oddly enough, the calls had been made while no one supposedly was living in the house. I grabbed a note pad from my handbag and wrote down all of the different numbers as well as the number from which the calls had been made.

I was going to destroy the original phone bill so I wouldn't be caught with the evidence of another broken law.

The second envelope contained the water bill. When I looked at the usage that was reported I was shocked. That empty house was consuming a lot more water than I was in my little happy home. What gives, I wondered?

Before I opened the third envelope, it came to mind that I ought to pick up my own mail. I sprang out of the car and walked up the street to my old, battered, and beaten mailbox where I snatched out the contents and ran back to the car. If anybody saw me doing that, they surely would know that Ellen Holcombe, fugitive from the law, was present and accounted for without question.

I threw my own mail onto the car seat nearly burying Nikki under the papers and drove off for fear that someone had spotted me.

A couple of blocks away I pulled over so I could finish scavenging through the envelopes. The same junk mail filled my mailbox that had filled Jonathan Smith's. I also received a telephone bill and water bill. Weren't we both so very, very lucky?

Most of my mail ended up being tossed into the back seat for further disposition at a later time. Finally I saw the third envelope that I had not opened from Jonathan Smith's mailbox.

When I took the time to look at the address on the front of the envelope I discovered that it was addressed to my attention.

"That's strange," I said to Nikki as I turned the envelope over in my hands trying to feel its contents. "Why would anybody address the letter to the little white house across the street and write my name on it? That just doesn't make any sense to me."

I slipped my finger into the corner of the flap and slid my finger across the backside of the envelope as I tried to open it without tearing it up as I had done with all of the other envelopes. This envelope was different because it didn't look like a bill as each of the other two had.

"Nikki, I wish I had a pot of boiling water so I could steam this open. Something tells me I'm not going to want to see what's inside."

Carefully I slid my finger trying not to destroy what may become evidence in my trial that was going to take place in my not too distant future. I silently chastised myself for not wearing gloves while I was stealing the mail.

The flap was finally removed and the contents of the envelope revealed what looked like the edge of a photograph that had been printed on regular paper by a color printer attached to a home computer. Again, I was sorry I wasn't wearing gloves but life goes on and I had to see what the picture was going to show me.

I sucked in a quick intake of air when I realized what I was holding onto.

"Oh, my God," I cried as I saw Eddy, Maggie, Barry, and Marty trussed up like Christmas turkeys. It wasn't a pleasant sight. As far as I could tell, because the photograph was not too distinct or clear, each one of the missing people were tied hand and foot with duct tape placed across their mouths.

Written at the bottom was:

If you say anything to the cops, FBI, or any type of law enforcement – they will die!!!!!!!!!!!!!!!!!!!!!!!!!!!!!

"Say what, Nikki? What is it that they don't want me to say?"

CHAPTER 21: PURSUED IN ERROR

Barry's car was no longer sitting on the curb where it had been parked. The police must have towed it. Why would they take Barry from me other than the fact that he was a cop? Was he getting too close to discovering who or what they were? Being a cop can lead you into trouble unawares.

Eddy, Maggie, and Marty weren't cops. Why were they gone?

Think, Ellen, think about why they wouldn't want you to talk. Think about why they have taken everyone except you.

In my heart I know that whatever was happening had something to do with that little white house across the street. But what? No one lived there, so I had been told. To tell you the truth, I hadn't seen anyone going in and out of that house except those four movers, the police officer, and that dark-haired woman that I didn't recognize. I didn't clearly see the faces of any of the six so I wouldn't be able to identify them to a soul. All I could remember about the movers was "Diamond Movers" emblazoned on their shirts and that they looked out of place. They definitely didn't look like the day laborers they should have been.

I was getting tired and my mind was fogging up from overwork and too much thinking. It was full dark and I needed some sleep. I grabbed Nikki and crawled into the back seat where I pulled her fuzzy blanket over the both of us so passersby couldn't tell we were in the car.

Sleep came in spurts, but I needed as much of it as I could get so I made myself stay in the back seat. I was crammed into a small space and I had pain from armrests and seat belts gouging into body parts.

Nikki rested fitfully, too. She would jump and shake with my every movement and any and all sounds she heard from outside of the car.

I rolled down both of the windows over the back seat about an inch to try to help the inside of the windows from steaming up caused by our breathing.

The night seemed unbearably long with my need to stay hidden. The pressure in my bladder became unbearable, too, so much so that I had to jump out of the car and sneak back into my house to relieve myself. Poor Nikki had to do her thing in the tall wet grass as she shook from the cold.

As I was leaving the house, two men dressed in dark suits sprang from the corner confronting me as soon as I locked the door. They had been waiting for me. I had no choice but to talk to them.

"Mrs. Holcombe, do you remember talking to us? Agents Thompson and Chandler. We need to ask you some more questions."

"What?" I sputtered in fright.

"We spoke with you about the little white house across the street."

"Oh yeah, I remember. What are you doing lurking around the corner trying to scare me half to death?" I asked harshly.

"We understand you are being sought by the town police. We wanted to talk to you without their interference, that's all. We could make a quick call. We have a radio in the car and I have a cell phone in my pocket. We could hold you and let them come get you. Would you prefer we do that or will you talk to us now and let us go on our way?"

"I always thought the law enforcement agencies worked together. Isn't that why we have Homeland Security? Why aren't you working with the town police? Why would you let me go?"

"Mrs. Holcombe, we have done some of our own investigating and we believe that you are being pursued in error. You are being questioned about the disappearance of a cop named Barry Johnson, aren't you?"

I nodded my head in answer.

"What about the other three people that everyone so conveniently forgets about? They have also disappeared. Do you believe I have anything to do with what has happened to them?"

"No ma'am, we don't."

"Why?"

"We aren't able to discuss that with you at this time."

"You've got to be kidding me!" I said in an incredulous tone surrounded wholeheartedly with sarcasm. "You can't tell me why I'm innocent of all of the charges the local police are trying to drum up against me. You aren't going to tell them either, are you?" I demanded with my voice beginning to crescendo.

"I'm sorry, Mrs. Holcombe, we are unable to help you at this time."

"Are you really FBI agents? Let me see your identification again," I demanded as I reached my hand forward to accept the proffered wallet.

I looked at it and could see nothing to indicate to me that they weren't FBI agents. I had called about them. I had been told there really was an Agent Thompson working out of the Richmond Office.

"Are you satisfied, Mrs. Holcombe?" asked Agent Thompson as he placed his wallet ID back into his inside breast pocket.

"You must put a lot of miles on your car. Oh, it's probably a company car, right?"

"Why would you ask that?"

"You aren't local. There is no local FBI office. The nearest one is Roanoke. How long does it take you to drive from Roanoke every time you want to talk to me?" I asked with a smile.

"Couple of hours. You've been to Roanoke. You know how far away it is and how long it takes to drive. Now, could we get on with the questions?"

"Sure," I said as I digested his words.

"Why don't we go inside?"

"I don't think I want to do that. If the locals see lights shining brightly, they might call the cops. You said you didn't want them involved, right?"

"Okay, I guess we can stand right here for the moment," said a reluctant Agent Thompson.

"What is it you want to know? I can't tell you very much about the little white house across the street, because I don't know anyone who lives there."

"Have you seen anyone go in and out of the house?"

"I believe I told you before that I saw four movers with "Diamond Movers" emblazoned on their shirts. I also saw a cop from the back. None of them were seen clearly enough by me to be recognizable."

"You've seen nothing else?"

"No. Should I have seen something? What is it I am supposed to have seen?"

"Nothing, nothing at all, if you are sure you have told me everything."

"Like I've said over and over again, I've seen a total of five people. I assume they were all men. The people that lived there moved out long before I saw the movers carrying in the new furniture. Whatever happened? I thought someone was moving in there. I hoped I was going to get new neighbors that were a little friendlier than the last couple."

"We can't say, Mrs. Holcombe."

"You can't? Or you won't? Which is it?"

"Does it matter?"

"No."

"I'm going to leave you my card. If you see anything new going on in or around that little white house across the street, please let me know."

"Sure, Agent Thompson, I hope your trip back to Roanoke is a pleasant one," I said sarcastically.

Agents Thompson and Chandler walked away from me and headed towards a nondescript gray sedan parked in front of my house.

As soon as they were in their vehicle, I raced to my car where I sat and stared at the darkness that was surrounding me. I roused myself from my hideaway world in my mind and starting verbalizing my thoughts.

"Nikki, I don't think they are real FBI agents. Or at the very least, they are corrupt FBI agents for whatever reason I don't know and understand. When I suggested their home base was Roanoke, they did not correct me. They should have told me they travel out of Richmond. Why did they lie to me?

"Why do they keep asking about the little white house across the street? What is it that I'm supposed to know about that house? If they are FBI agents, why aren't they watching that house? What is going on in that house? I know there is someone living there. I may not have seen them come and go, but the phone bill and the water bill tell me a different tale.

"I forgot to tell them about the brown-haired guy that Maggie saw the first time I talked to them. I didn't tell them this time, on purpose; and, I didn't mention the woman.

"I've got to get into that house without getting myself killed or snatched and tortured. I've got to get my family and my friends back from the claws of the freaks who have snatched them from my life. I want to go home, Nikki," I said as I cuddled my Chihuahua in my arms.

CHAPTER 22: SINGING THE SIREN SONG

I had my head down snuggling my face into the welcoming warmth of Nikki when I noticed a flash of light behind me. I tensed immediately because Nikki and I weren't hiding. We were not cowering underneath the shield of her fuzzy blanket to hide us both from prying eyes. It was too late to lay myself down against the seat. I was sure the driver behind the headlights would have seen me in all of my ignorance as I was sitting upright on my seat without a care in the world.

The lights shone brightly behind me but they were not moving. What did that mean? Was the driver exiting from his car to come accost me and my little dog?

I looked into my rearview mirror and saw nothing but the bright headlights that were forcing the surroundings to look even darker and blacker than they already were during this cloud covered night.

I saw no one walking up to my car. All I could see were bright lights.

"Hang on, Nikki, we're out of here," I said as I turned the ignition and stomped on the gas pedal almost simultaneously.

I drove as if Satan himself were after me. Those bright headlights were right behind me, keeping pace with me without hesitation.

"I can't see who is driving, Nikki. I don't know if it's a police vehicle, or not."

No sirens were activated, no flashing lights were switched on, but the vehicle kept coming after me. I was afraid I wouldn't be able to lose the vehicle this time. Even though the night was dark and there were many places to hide, I couldn't get far enough away from the vehicle to build any kind of barrier between my car and his.

"What should I do, Nikki?"

Nikki was hunkered down in the front seat. She knew there was danger behind us as well as in front of us.

I suddenly turned right onto a country road that led out behind the new dam. Maybe whoever was following didn't know the area, especially if it wasn't a cop. I extinguished the lights on my vehicle and drove ahead into the darkness. If I could make out some of the dark shadows along the route, I knew I would be able to stay on the road.

The headlights behind me took on the appearance of being further back than they originally were.

"I think it's working, Nikki. If I can keep this car on the road, I think I can lose the tail," I whispered as I glanced into the rearview mirror at every opportunity I could find and still stay on the road.

228

I took another right turn that took me completely off the road. I followed the gravel road around a creek bank to a small bridge where I crossed over to get to the picnic area and a couple of small dark buildings that I could hide behind. I was so thankful for the times that I had picnicked with my sons and their friends when they were younger. That was the only reason I knew about this hiding place.

"Nikki, I think that was our so-called FBI agents. They aren't very good at their jobs are they?" I asked as a smile sneaked up to the corners of my mouth.

I hid behind one of the dark storage buildings with all car lights extinguished and I discovered that I was actually holding my breath so whoever my stalker was couldn't hear me. My eyes were darting around but all I could see was darkness. Darkness was good, that meant that whoever was on my trail had lost it.

When I thought the coast was clear, I drove slowly from my hiding place, without the benefit of headlights, and headed back towards the little white house across the street.

The thought of going to that house was upper most in my mind. I was being drawn there like metal filings to a magnet.

It was still dark which was helpful because I wanted to park Eddy's car on the street and walk to the house where I intended to get inside any way that I could. I was going to find out why that house was singing its siren song, guiding me to its interior.

The neighborhood was quiet, too quiet for my comfort. I had the feeling of the calm before the storm. I was afraid I was going to be the storm.

"Nikki, old girl, I'm going to get some answers tonight, I guess I should say this morning, or I'm going to die trying," I said to my beloved pet. "I don't know what I would do without you to keep me on the straight and narrow."

I parked the car in front of my house. It was Eddy's car. Maybe the neighbors wouldn't remember what kind of car Eddy drove and guess that I was driving it now.

"Nikki, you've got to stay in the car. I'm going to leave it unlocked just in case something happens to me. I want someone to be able to rescue you if I don't get back here," I said as I stroked my little dog while tears rolled down my cheeks.

When I exited the car, I stood up straight; I was determined to show no fear. My knees were jelly and my heart was beating like a bass drum, but I wanted to show no fear. Did I expect there to be an audience? Yes, I did. I don't think I had done anything for the last few days that wasn't under constant scrutiny. By, whom? The so-called FBI agents, of course.

I could hear Nikki whining. How odd, Nikki almost never whined when I left her. She must have felt my tension and anxiety.

"It's okay, girl. I promise I will be back and we will go home where I'll get my front door fixed and we can grow old together," I whispered as I continued to walk toward the little white house across the street.

CHAPTER 23: NIKKI WAS GONE

I walked right up to the front door and started knocking. It was four o'clock in the morning but the time of day didn't matter to me. The gentle knocking achieved no results so I balled up my fist and started pounding.

"Is anybody home in there?" I asked the closed door.

No lights were flipped on and no footsteps could be heard racing to the front door. After waiting a few more moments, I scurried down the front steps that were actually the back steps and walked around the house to the back of the house that was actually the front.

"Hey, is anyone in there," I shouted as I beat on the door with my fist.

Again no signs of life were displayed, not within my line of vision. I walked back down the steps and started walking around the house looking at the brick foundation. I was looking for basement windows through which I could see the dark interior. I located one on the right side of the house but when I dropped down to my knees to get a better look, I saw that the inside of the window had been painted black to allow no unwanted observers. I hurried around to the left side of the house where I located a second basement window. It, too, was blacked out.

"Well, I know you're hiding something," I mumbled as I walked to what I considered the front of the house and started searching under shrubbery and mud mats for a hidden key. I brought my flashlight with me just for the help in snooping for a key. I upturned all the rocks and bricks that were scattered in the front yard close to the house hoping the key had been hidden in an obvious place.

"Nothing here, I'll go around again and see what's out back or front or whatever," I whispered knowing full well that if anyone saw me searching the bushes and porches I would be arrested with no questions asked. Not only would they arrest me for the obvious intent to enter a domain that wasn't my own, but the men with the special white coats wouldn't be far behind because of all of the conversations I was holding with myself.

Under any bushes and shrubs nothing was hidden, but under the bottom wooden porch step, I found a shiny, bight key that actually hadn't been hidden very well, not well at all. It was like they wanted me to find it. Perhaps they did. Oh well, now that I had it, should I go into the house? Should I plow headlong into the trouble waiting inside? Of course, I should. Why the heck would I be here if that wasn't the plan?

I shoved the key into my pocket for safe keeping. I needed to check on my Nikki.

I glanced around me. I could see the first signs of daylight as the darkness seemed to thin out a little bit. I walked to the car and peeked inside.

No Nikki.

Maybe she managed to squeeze her little body under the seat.

"Nikki, come here. Here, Nikki, come on out," I said anxiously.

Nikki was gone. She didn't whimper to let me know that she might be stuck under the seat. Someone had taken my precious dog.

"Who would do that?" I cried.

I had seen no one as I searched the shrubbery and bushes of the little white house across the street. Of course, it would have been easy not to see anyone when I had the house between me and the roadway. But, I didn't hear anyone either - no footsteps, no crunching gravel. That could be explained by the person wearing rubber soled shoes and that same person walking only on the grass.

The more excuses I was making for the ghostly disappearance of my dog only served to make me angrier with each one that I fabricated in my mind. Nikki was the last straw. Taking her away from me was like taking my heart out of my chest. The pain was almost as strong, no it was as strong, as the pain of losing my husband. Nikki had covered the hole in my heart that his death had created.

I knew Nikki wouldn't have allowed anyone to pick her up without a fight. She was a tiny dog but she had razor sharp teeth and a bad temper when she was cornered. I hoped she had taken a chunk out of the dognapper. I could almost bet that she did.

I looked up and down the street and saw no other cars that didn't belong there. I made myself listen intently. I wanted to hear the tiny squeaky sounds of my frightened Chihuahua.

Nothing – no dog sounds.

I did hear a hum, a distant hum that I hadn't heard before. It probably had been there all along, I just hadn't paid any attention to it. Maybe that hum meant something. Maybe that hum could lead me to some answers. It sounded like a motor of some kind like a heat pump motor except that it was a heavier, deeper sound. It wasn't the tinny sounds of a single residential heat pump motor running. It sounded much bigger, more muffled. It was like whoever installed it didn't want anyone to hear it. That would have probably been the case except that I was straining every nerve in my body to hear a sound from Nikki.

The trees behind the little white house across the street seemed to be part of the protective covering for the hum. I never noticed that before, either. I was going to have to start looking around more and taking into my memory what I see or don't see and what I hear and don't hear.

I walked slowly towards the hum.

When I reached the trees, I realized why I hadn't noticed any strange contraption hidden among them. There was a tall fence almost as tall as the trees and about the same color of green as the pine needles on the evergreens that had to be several years old in order to reach the stately heights they had grown to.

It had to be a huge heat pump or maybe more than one. It must be pumping air in and out of a massive area. It was much too large to be a heat source for a single residence judging by the size of the enclosure.

I walked around the trees so I could find a way to get over or under the fence. The thought of finding a gate that would allow me to walk through it seemed out of the question. The stand of trees had hidden the fence so well that that was all I thought it had been – a stand of trees that someone had left on their property to permit the land owner to think he was communing with nature. I managed to force my not so small body through the closely growing trees so I could get a good view of every part of the tall, very tall, green fence.

I did find a gate with a great, big, huge padlock attached to it. I guess they didn't want snoops like me getting inside the green fence to see what was causing the hum.

Unless I climbed a tree which was not, and I emphasize not, going to happen, I was going to have to resign myself to allowing the hum to remain an actual mystery for the moment. My guesses about the purpose of the enclosed machinery would have to remain guesses.

The fence was not new but it was well taken care of. When I touched it, I discovered that what I thought was wood was actually metal. It had to have been there for quite a while because the trees growing next to it were gigantic.

My next thought was to see if there were any cables stretching from a utility pole to the fence and to whatever was humming. I looked skyward and saw no electrical hookups of any kind leading to the area of the fence. Must be underground cabling. If so, it has been there for a while. I could find no recently disturbed ground anywhere near the trees or fence.

This wasn't getting me anywhere.

I reached inside my pocket and pulled out the bright, shiny key that I had discovered earlier. I walked to the door where I thought the key would fit. I slid the key into the lock and turned it slowly so as not to cause any noise.

The key fit without a problem into the slot but it wouldn't operate the tumblers. It was either the wrong key or the wrong door.

I stepped off the porch at the back/front of the house and peered around the side looking for nosy neighbors. It never occurred to me that I was one of those people I was trying to hide from. Me – a nosy neighbor, never.

I hurried around to the other end of the house, the one facing the street and my house, where I slowly climbed up the steps to the porch. I inserted the key and turned it whispering "please work – please work – please work" until I felt the tumblers give and start to turn. I really hadn't expected that to happen. Even though I prayed that it would, I hadn't expected it to be that easy.

I turned the door knob and pushed the door open slightly. I heard a noise. It sounded like something running and scratching its claws against the wooden floor.

"Rats," I said a little too loudly as I pushed the door open wider so I could see the gray monster crawl under the worn out old sofa pushed against the wall. It was almost full daylight so the door being opened wider allowed enough light to enter the room to let me know that no one was there, except the rat.

The room was dusty and disheveled and definitely didn't look lived in. That is to say that no one had dusted or vacuumed for several days perhaps even months.

I walked through what I considered the living room to the next room leading to the other end of the house. It was a dining room that I was standing in that also needed a good cleaning. No one had been disturbing the dust around these two rooms for months even though I knew I had seen people go in and out of this house within the last couple of weeks. There had to be some sign of dust disturbance but I couldn't find any, not in these two rooms.

I continued on to where I thought the end of the house would be. That's where I found the kitchen. Unlike the rest of the house, the kitchen was spotlessly clean. All metal shined brightly and what was supposed to be white was white. It didn't make any sense. Why would this room be clean as a whistle when all the others were just shy of being dump worthy?

I slid open a drawer of the spotless built-in cabinets to check to see if the inside was as clean as the outside appeared to be.

Nothing there and it was clean.

The second drawer was also spotlessly clean.

The third and bottom drawer was a duplicate of the first two with one difference. There was a large brown envelope inside the drawer pushed as far back as they could make it go.

I tugged at the brown envelope freeing it from the drawer and pulled the flap back so I could see the contents.

It looked like airline tickets, six of them, for three different locations with departures set for the next day. I wanted to take each ticket out and look for a name, but I knew I didn't have time. The only one I actually had taken the time to read was a ticket made out to Mary Smith.

It took a real imagination to come up with that name, I guess.

I was running out of time. I could feel it in my bones.

I heard a noise.

I couldn't tell what the sound was, but I didn't want to take any more time looking at the airline tickets and not the rest of the house.

I shoved the airline tickets back into the envelope, placed that same envelope into the back of the drawer trying to make it look as though it had not been touched.

My mind started sending me little warnings that I began to pay attention to for fear of being one of the lost which now included my dog, Nikki. Nikki was the last straw. You'd think the loss of four people would have pushed me forward for answers but that didn't happen. It was beginning to wear on me, their loss, I mean, but being human beings, a thought that lingered in my failing brain was that maybe they wanted to be lost. I didn't want to believe that but it was hovering around the edges. I wanted them to be found because they wanted to found. I didn't want to know anything different. I worried about them all, especially my son, Eddy. I wanted Eddy back where I could call him and talk to him and let him know that he was loved.

Now Nikki was a different matter. She was a helpless, defenseless, tiny dog.

THEY SHOULDN'T HAVE TAKEN MY DOG.

CHAPTER 24: WILD-EYED AND STRANGE

The nagging little warnings that were flashing through my brain were telling me to protect myself. I had no gun. That was a fact for sure. I needed something to throw, or stab, or swing, or all three if someone or something came at me with malice aforethought.

I looked around the sparkling kitchen for some kind of weapon. What could I use? I found a knife but it was only a small paring size. I shoved that into my breast pocket of my shirt with the point sticking upward.

I opened and closed more of the drawers as quietly as I could as I searched for something else; a hammer perhaps or something with heft that might draw blood if I could swing it hard enough. I opened and closed cabinet doors and finally spotted a large cast iron skillet. You'd better believe that sucker was heavy. If I could get enough momentum behind it as I swung it at an attacker, the skillet could easily become a deadly weapon.

I knew I was beginning to look a little wild-eyed and strange as I carried in my left hand a heavy cast iron skillet and poking from my breast pocket the dangerous end of a paring knife. That doesn't even take into account that my clothes were wrinkled and lived in because of my wallowing around in the car. It also overlooks the fact that fear forms an odor that isn't too very pleasant but I was on the hunt for answers. I was going to get those answers one way or another.

Well, I had traveled through a living room, a dining room, and a kitchen; now I needed to check the rooms that branched off the main line from one end of the house to the other.

Back to the living room I slowly crept so as not to allow heavy footsteps to break the silence that surrounded me. I couldn't even hear the hum that had driven me here in the first place. Off the living room was a bedroom that was dusty and dirty and not a welcoming sight for my exhausted, old body. I saw a dresser with a dirty mirror that was attached to a life worn set of drawers encased in old mahogany colored wood. I pulled the top drawer open and found small bits of paper in the bottom of it. The second drawer was showing me the same paper except it had the addition of mouse droppings for extra appeal.

"Yuck," I said as I slid the drawer back to its original position.

I wasn't sure whether I wanted to look into the third drawer or not. I did and it contained paper and droppings also. I was so relieved when nothing sprang out at me to scare the life out of me.

I opened the closet to see a few scattered metal hangers and nothing more than dust and spider webs.

There was a door leading from that bedroom that connected to a small bathroom. From that small bathroom that offered no clues other than deep red rust stains and grime on the sink and bathtub, I entered another bedroom that appeared to branch off of the dining room. It contained the same type of furniture except that the wood color was a little lighter, perhaps a walnut. The dresser drawers contained the paper nesting materials of mice along with the droppings for added measure.

"They need to get rid of the rodents," I mumbled in disgust.

I walked through the dining room and returned to the kitchen where I opened a door that led to what appeared to be a pantry. All of the shelves were empty except for one lonely can of pinto beans. I reached up and pulled on the can of beans.

A clicking and whirring sound started up and the pantry shelves moved back away from me. I stood there watching with the heavy cast iron skillet at the ready for whatever was going to jump out at me.

There was a strong puff of cool almost cold but fresh air that escaped from the area on the other side of the pantry shelf. What I could see from where I was standing was dimly lit and appeared to be a set of steps leading to a basement or cellar.

"Pretty fancy door to only go to the basement," I mumbled as I stepped forward through the opening.

I carried my weapon, the cast iron skillet, in my left hand so I used my right hand to help guide me down the steps. I placed my hand gently against the dirty, webby bricks to steady myself and progressed down each step slowly and gently to make as little noise as possible. I strained my hearing to the point that I was sure I could hear spiders crawling on the staircase, but nothing else. No other sounds were filtering through. I thought that was odd. I should hear sounds of water dripping and the house creaking and sighing. But – I heard nothing.

My nerves were taunt like a spring wound too tight and I was sure I was going to uncoil with the slightest bit of fright. I pressed forward away from the wooden steps and into the dark, damp, musty, brick lined basement room.

If there were rats and mice upstairs, the basement ought to hold the real monsters of the rodent world.

"Stop thinking about rats," I told myself as I slid my feet forward. I was afraid to actually pick my feet up because of the noise that would be generated when I slapped my foot down against the floor. If I lifted my foot only a fraction of an inch or so and slid it forward without it touching the surface of the basement floor, I thought the noise would be much less.

I took the flashlight I had stuffed into my pants pocket and ignited the light knowing full well that the illumination would not be seen from outside because the windows were blacked out with paint.

The sudden brightness startled me for a moment and I very nearly dropped the heavy cast iron skillet. That clatter of cast iron hitting concrete floor would have raised the dead. I had no doubt about that.

"Steady, Ellen, let your eyes focus," I told myself as I stood still, closed my eyes, and drew in a heavy breath. I exhaled slowly, opened my eyes, and discovered that I could see most of the room except for the black corners, if that's what they were. I would have to walk closer to the blackness to know for sure.

The basement appeared to be much smaller than the house, that is, if my depth perception was correct.

"There's got to be more to this basement or cellar or whatever this underground hole in the earth is," I said as I stepped towards the blackest of the corners.

The closer I moved to the blackness, the easier it was to distinguish another doorway. There was no light at all emanating from the doorway so I was in desperate need of the flashlight that seemed to be dimming from constant use.

I shook the flashlight and whispered, "You had better stay with me, light. I need all the help I can get." With the last forceful shake, the circle of light displayed on the floor appeared to be just a little bit brighter.

That doorway led to another stairway which common sense would tell me should lead up. No – this one went down to another level beneath the basement level I was already searching. "A sub-basement, those only exist in movies as far as I know, not a private residence, especially this private residence," I mumbled as I started to descend the steps.

I was scared when I started this searching business, but now, I was beyond scared. I had no idea what I was getting into with my traipsing down these steps into the unknown.

My descent was slow because I was trying to check out everything within my limited sight line that consisted of a small circle of light emitted from my flashlight with batteries that were beginning to weaken from over use.

There was nothing particularly interesting about the stairway except that it was a stairway leading to another basement. At the bottom, no more than three feet from the last stair tread was a door.

The door was locked.

I put my ear up against the door and I could hear the hum, the very same hum I had heard outside of the house that was coming from the green fenced in area. The enclosed monstrosity outside was the ventilation system for this underground piece of hell. I had to get to the other side of this door. I knew that was where my missing family and friends were being held, hopefully, still alive.

I reached my hand over my head to feel around the door facing for a hidden key.

"God, I wish I didn't have to stick my hand up there," I prayed fearing the spiders and all of the other creepy crawlies that lived in the earth. I felt around every area that was within my reach. I was about to give up when my flashlight reflected off of a shiny object secreted between two bricks where the mortar had been scraped out for that purpose.

The hiding place was about eye level for me, I guess that's why I caught the glint because I was swinging my flashlight around while I was reaching up over the door hunting a key.

"Thank you, Lord," I whispered as I worked the key from between the two bricks.

CHAPTER 25: I WAS BEING WATCHED

The key slipped into the slot located on the doorknob. While turning the key, it turned the doorknob and allowed access to the other side. Before I pushed the door open far enough to enter the mysterious other side, I wanted to take a deep breath. As I exhaled, I entered into the unknown, again.

Then there was light – that's how I felt when I walked through that door. I had been feeling my way through the dark for so long, that a forty watt light bulb would have been more than welcome. As it turned out, I was walking under fluorescent lights that illuminated a hallway leading, of course, to another door.

My skin started to crawl. I felt as if I were being watched by many sets of eyes. I looked up, down, side to side, and behind me but I couldn't find a camera. I looked at the walls, perhaps these were one way viewing windows. They were dark walls; I really couldn't determine the color. I knew I couldn't see beyond the wall, but I had no way of knowing if someone on the other side could see me walking down the hall. I had a feeling deep in my gut that I was being watched through both walls on either side of the hallway.

When I got to the door, since I knew my presence was known, I didn't bother to knock or even try to hide the fact that I was entering into their domain.

"Welcome, Mrs. Holcombe. We are glad to see you," said a sarcastic voice from the shadows of the room I had entered.

"You seem to know who I am. Who are you?" I demanded.

"In due time, we will tell you in due time," snapped back the rapid response.

"Where is my son? My friends Barry, Maggie, and her son Marty, where are they? What have you done with them?" I demanded. I didn't know where I found the nerve to do that, demand an answer I mean, because I was scared to death.

"All of your lives will return to normal in a couple of days. But, until then you will have to remain here."

"Where is my dog?"

"Look under the counter on the other side of the room. She has been sedated. She will awaken shortly. I expect you to keep her quiet. Do you understand?"

"Aw, Nikki," I cried as I looked at my little Chihuahua. She was breathing. She was alive. He hadn't killed her, not yet anyway.

"You will be able to join the others shortly. But first, we have a few questions for you to answer."

246

"What about?"

"This house and those who have lived here over the years."

"I don't know anything about this house and the people who have lived here."

"Don't lie to us, Mrs. Holcombe."

"What do you want me to tell you then? What is it you think I know?"

"That's what you have to tell me, Mrs. Holcombe."

"Tell you and who else? Which one are you, Agent Thompson or Agent Chandler? I can't tell from this distance and not being able to see your face."

"Who are Agent Thompson and Agent Chandler?"

"One of them is you, that's who. Now, please tell me."

"Now, Mrs. Holcombe, I want you to tell me about anyone you have seen go in or out of that house over the entire time you have lived across the street."

"You've got to be kidding, Agent Chandler. It has to be you. I would recognize Thompson's voice because he was the one who always did the talking. You guys know that I work for a living. I, therefore, have not been home a lot. Thus, I couldn't tell you about the comings and goings in the little white house across the street."

"You've got to do better than that, Mrs. Holcombe."

"Detective Green, is that who you are? Are you the cop who has been trying to run me into the ground?"

"Mrs. Holcombe, you are avoiding answering my questions. I can't have that, Mrs. Holcombe. We will be forced to induce you to talk to us by hurting someone. Do you want that to happen, Mrs. Holcombe? Do you want us to hurt your friend Maggie?"

"How do I know you haven't killed her already? I haven't seen her for days. Why did you take her?"

"She saw something she shouldn't have seen. We had to keep her under wraps so she wouldn't tell anybody about it."

"Is she still alive?"

"Sure she is, but she will be damaged soon if you don't tell us what we need to know."

"Prove it to me. I need to know that she is okay?"

"Mrs. Holcombe, the hallway that you walked through to get to me allowed me to see you from this side. The other side allows your missing friends and family to see you. They all know you are here. They will also know immediately whether or not you are cooperating. They each told me what they knew about the house. You are the only one remaining. If you don't tell me what I need to know, you will all die. Do you understand?"

"Can I sit down?" I said weakly. "I feel like I'm going to faint right out."

"Behind you, there's a chair."

"I don't see it......" I said as I crumpled to the floor.

"Are you ready to get up yet?" asked the voice.

I didn't answer. I wanted him to offer to help me by walking to me to help me up off of the floor. I wanted to see who I was talking with so I could possibly reason out this whole mess.

"Mrs. Holcombe, you are really a clever lady. I know that. But your little trick will not work with me. You need to get up all by yourself. I will not help you," he said angrily.

I didn't move. My face was not positioned towards his sight line. He couldn't see that I was fully alert and awake. I laid there without moving a muscle.

"Mrs. Holcombe, we will stay right here until you come to your senses. Please get up and answer my questions."

A few more seconds passed and then I decided I had better start stirring around. My old bones were not handling the hard floor very well. I had to get up and move to ease some of the pain.

"Mrs. Holcombe."

"Yes."

"There is a chair behind you. Go to it and sit down. Don't try to trick me again. It won't work."

"What is it you want, Agent Chandler?"

"What is the information you have about this house?"

"All I can do is tell you what I've found out recently? Is that what you want?"

"That will do for starters."

"How long will it be before my Nikki wakes up? I would like to hold her."

"Not until you talk to us?"

"Us? Is someone here with you?"

"No."

"You said us?"

"My mistake."

"This house belongs to Jonathan Smith out of Alexandria, Virginia. I have no idea why Jonathan Smith would want this house in this small town away from the outside world. In truth, there probably is no Jonathan Smith connected with the purchase of this house except in name only. I know that the water usage in this empty house is more than the average usage for a family of four. I know that I saw four movers with the name "Diamond Movers" written on their shirts. They moved in a bunch of new furniture. I also know that the furniture upstairs isn't what was moved into this house. I know I saw a police officer enter this house. I know that my friend, Maggie, saw a man leaving this house and I saw a woman. We could not identify anybody. I know that the previous inhabitants were named Brown and they are having their mail forwarded to a detective by the name of Green. I swear to you that's all I know."

"Where did you get all of this information?"

"Why?"

"We need to know. If you can find out all of this and you're not a professional, others can do that same thing."

"Maybe, maybe not?"

"What do you mean by that?"

"I had to deceive a few people to get some answers. Someone might say that I broke a few laws but I did it anyway."

"Those movers, Mrs. Holcombe, did you get a good look at them?"

"No, it was at night. I couldn't see their faces."

"How did you read the logo "Diamond Movers" if it was that dark?"

"It was written in white letters against a dark background. It was also on the back of their shirts which made it pretty large to begin with, you know how they use large letters on the back of shirts to advertise."

"Mrs. Holcombe, what else do you know?"

"Nothing that I can think of at this moment. I swear I don't remember anything else. Why don't you let us go?"

"Soon, Mrs. Holcombe, soon, as long as you cooperate. Your friends and family were caught in the same trap you wandered into but they got here much quicker than you did. They plunged ahead with the snooping first and planned to ask questions later. You did the complete opposite so you were a little more knowledgeable about the whole situation."

"What kind of place is this? Why does this house have two basements?"

"That's simple enough to answer. The man who originally built this place was a wee bit eccentric as well as paranoid. He thought the Russians were going to drop an Atomic Bomb on this tiny town so he built the subbasement as a bomb shelter. It turned out to be a good place to work for us in our endeavors."

"And they are?" I questioned as I looked for an explanation.

"The less you know about our plans, the more likely you are to survive this ordeal, Mrs. Holcombe."

"Please let us go! If we promise not to tell anybody what happened or where you are, will you let us all go?"

"I'm afraid not. We've got one more task ahead of us. Then you can leave."

"How long will that be?"

"Tomorrow."

CHAPTER 26: TOMORROW

Tomorrow – that's not so long. I can last that long.

I heard a whimper and knew that Nikki was finally coming out of her sedation. I walked over to the cage where I could see her starting to move around a bit.

"Nikki, come here, girl. It's me, Nikki. Come on over here. I'll hold you. I swear I won't let the mean man bother you again," I said as I snatched her from the cage and held her in my arms.

Nikki raised her head slowly and loved me back with the gentle touch of her tongue against my cheek.

Tears were rolling down my cheeks. I was so glad to hold and feel the unconditional love that this tiny defenseless creature was giving to me.

"Mrs. Holcombe?"

"Yes."

"You will need to stay in this room with your snappy little dog until we have completed our task."

"What about the others? Why can't I stay with them?"

"I believe you will be a formidable disruption. They have been worn down and forced to succumb to my suggestions. You have not. I do not want you joining them at this time."

"Can I, at least, see them? I need to know they are all right."

"There is a door with a piece of something that looks like painted glass in it. Go to it and turn the small knob you will find off to the left at the top of that door."

I walked slowly to where he said I should go as I held tightly to Nikki. When I turned the knob at the top of the door, I could see them, all of them. They were bound hand and foot onto chairs that were placed directly in front of what must have been the hallway that led me to this room.

They are alive. All of them are alive.

"Let us out of here!" I screamed.

No response. I was not told to shut up or threatened in any way. I believed he was gone. My captor was not here. Where did he go? How did he get out?

I left the window view open so those on the other side of that door could see me if they were interested. I started searching again. That seemed to be all I was doing lately – searching.

There must have been a hidden panel, someplace where my captor slipped through and away back into the free world. I looked the room over but I couldn't find it. If it was there, it must have had access from the other side or it was controlled with a remote.

I walked to the door where I had entered the room. It was locked, but I still had the key. I automatically jerked it out of the knob when I entered the room so I would be able to get back out. My guard must not have seen that little move or he would have removed the key from my possession.

I unlocked the door and found my way back up to the first basement level, then slowly felt my way up in the darkness to the house level. I needed to get some help. If I called the police I was afraid they would lock me up without listening to me.

"Okay, Nikki, what can we do? Who can we call?"

I ran out of the house, to Eddy's car that was still parked on the street. I climbed into the vehicle and sat there.

"Where am I going to go? Not to the police – where?" I cried as I placed my head against the steering wheel for a few moments.

I exited the car and walked boldly and proudly to my house, to the rear door because the front door was still nailed shut. I picked up the telephone and dialed the school board office.

"May I speak with Sylvia, please?"

"May I tell her who is calling?" asked a sweet sounding voice.

"Ellen Holcombe."

"One moment, please."

There was a pause, a long pause, because I knew by saying my name, it would cause an uproar. I was beginning to wonder if Sylvia was going to speak to me when the silence was interrupted.

"Ellen?"

"Sylvia?"

"Yes, Ellen, what do you want?"

"You can, at the very least, be civil, Sylvia. All I want you to do is call the police and ask them to meet me at 302 Valleyview Street where I will surrender to them. Can you do that for me?"

"You can do it yourself. I don't want to get involved."

"Sorry, old friend, but you are involved because you are such a gooooood friend to me."

"I'm going to hang up."

"Go ahead, Sylvia. Then you'll have to explain why you wouldn't cooperate with the police. See the police might get the idea that you have been helping me all along. Who's to say that you weren't?"

"Where do you want the police to meet you?" she demanded angrily.

"At 302 Valleyview Street, the little white house across the street from my house. That's all you need to tell them except that they need to go to the back of the house into the kitchen and down to the basement. That's where I'll be. Can you remember that, old friend?"

"I'm not stupid, Ellen."

"You could have fooled me," I said as I hung up the telephone.

I knew it wouldn't take long for the sirens to be wailing so at the first sign of a distant squeal I ran across the street with Nikki under my arm and waited next to the back door of the house. My fear now was that my captor would return before the sirens arrived at my meeting. I couldn't have that. How would I be able to lead the police to the others if he arrived first?

I heard a noise that seemed to be coming from the confines of the green fence. It was him. I knew deep down in my gut that it was him. There must have been another way out of the bomb shelter within the area confined by the green fence.

I knew the fence was padlocked from the outside, so, again, he must have a hidden exit controlled by some kind of touch panel or remote so he could get out into the real world. If that was the case, I was in real trouble. I could be seen from the fenced area as I stood near the back door of the little white house across the street.

"Nikki, you're going to have to help me. I know you're scared. So am I," I said as I softly spoke to my dog and stroked her to let her know how much I loved her. "When I put you down on the ground, I want you to go to the front of house and lead the policemen back to me. Meanwhile, I'll try to lead my prison guard on just enough of a chase to get him into the hallway with me and the police. Hopefully, no one will get hurt, especially you and me."

The sound of the sirens must have hastened my captor to finish whatever it was that he was doing because he suddenly appeared on my side of the green fence and I was looking straight at him, Agent Chandler in all of his glory.

I quickly put Nikki on the ground and shooed her towards the front of the house while I veered towards a neighbor's house where I knew there would be no one at home.

"Go, Nikki, go, girl!" I shouted as I ran.

He came after me like I knew he would.

I had to be a comical sight as I forced my short legs to propel my overweight body much faster than my age and condition allowed. I ran like Satan was chasing me.

I swerved again, even though it was actually bringing me closer to my pursuer, so I could get the attention of the police cars that were racing up the street towards the house. My pursuer caught sight of the police cars and he backed off a little allowing me to run around to the back of the house as I called for Nikki.

Nikki met me at the back door where I paused long enough for me to snatch her from the ground and proceed inside the house. Once inside I waited until I heard several sets of footsteps. Then I raced down the first flight of steps. Again, I paused. I didn't want to lose the police. Not after I finally got them here to help.

When I caught sight of the feet of the first cop coming after me, I yelled, "This way," and ran down the second flight of steps.

Then all chasing stopped. Why?

The smell, I could smell gas coming from the lower level.

"He's killing them! Help me get them out of there!" I shouted as I raced to the door and unlocked it.

Inside the room I grabbed a chair and pushed it into the hallway where I crashed it through the side of the room where they were being held - all four of them.

Finally, a policeman came forward and helped me drag them out to the air. I was afraid the place would blow up before we all could get out of there.

"Hurry, please, hurry. My son is unconscious and so is Maggie. Please hurry!" I screamed as the policemen worked as fast as they could cutting them loose from their bindings and carrying or helping them up the two flights of steps to the wonderful gasless, clean air of a beautiful morning.

CHAPTER 27: ARRESTED

I was arrested.

No surprise. I knew I would be.

"Mrs. Holcombe, you broke every law short of murder in your pursuit of your so-called truth," said the angry chief of police as he tugged at his short shirt sleeve to cover that ugly bruise and cuts on his upper arm.

"Yes sir, but you weren't going to help me find my family and friends. You thought I was the one who did something to them. At least, that's what you wanted me to believe," I responded just as angrily.

"You went about this in the wrong way. You should have turned yourself in so we could help."

"Yeah, right."

"You need to cooperate with us, Mrs. Holcombe. Maybe we can get the charges dropped if you will tell us everything that happened."

"Like what? What do you want to know?"

"Who was the man holding everyone captive?"

"I don't know."

"But you talked to him, didn't you?"

"Yes, but he was in the shadows. All I can do is hazard a guess."

"All right, guess."

"Do you have a Detective Green on your police force?"

"Yes."

"You might want to find out why the mail from that house at 302 Valleyview Street was being forwarded to him."

"Go on."

"I was questioned a few times, I think it was three times, but everything is getting jumbled up in my mind right now, by two so-called FBI Agents named Thompson and Chandler. I don't think they are FBI. I think they are from your police force, too, just like Green."

"Those are strong accusations to be making about law enforcement officers."

"Yes sir, I know that. But as I pieced the puzzle together, that was the only solution I could come up with. There is still a piece missing."

"Really?"

"The men who moved the furniture into the house from "Diamond Movers" were members of your police force and bank robbers. There were four of them. I don't know who the fourth person is.

"I believe I saw him enter the house alone at a later date but I didn't get a good look at him. I only saw him from the back and he was dressed in a uniform like you and all the other cops. I believe Maggie saw the same man one other time leaving the house.

"The man who held me captive said there was one more task to do. I'm sure he meant one more task other than killing us captives."

"What would that task have been?"

"They had to move the furniture back out before they blew up the house."

"Why on earth would they have to do that?"

"That's where the stolen money, gold, and jewelry are hidden."

"I'll have to do some investigating. If your story checks out, I will let you return home. By the way, your son has your little dog. He wanted me to tell you that so you wouldn't worry."

I was led away and pushed back into the holding cell after I was searched by the dark-haired female police officer who looked vaguely familiar. I guess it was déjà vu all over again.

How long was I going to have to endure this punishment for having done the right thing? If I hadn't broken every law under the sun, Eddy, Marty, Maggie, and Barry would all be dead. Of course, Nikki and I would have been dead, too. There was no way I would be left alive to point the way to the little white house across the street.

Suddenly my mind flashed back to the ugly bruise and cuts on the chief's arm. Nikki did that. She actually bit the chief. Good for her.

The chief of police was not going to be grateful that I had done his job. He was not embarrassed because the task was accomplished by a civilian, on the contrary. He was unhappy for a totally different reason.

I was worried because now I knew who the fourth man was and I had no way in the world to let anybody know before I was eliminated as a problem. How I was going to be eliminated, I didn't have a clue. My mysterious death would probably be reported to the media as a suicide.

My only hope for a long lasting life would be if Barry returned to work soon, very soon.

The night was long and agonizing because I had to force myself to stay awake. I was not going to go gentle into the goodnight - not for anybody. They were going to have to take me from this world kicking and screaming if I had any say in the matter.

I paced the tiny cell until my legs drove me down onto the cot due to the constant pain shooting up my extremities. I knew the pain would keep me awake if nothing else could.

I glanced at my watch and saw that it was time for the shift to change. Maybe Barry would come in to work, or maybe he would want to check on me, if he wasn't able to work yet which was something I didn't know for sure. I didn't want to ask the chief because I was afraid he would discourage Barry from coming in at all.

"Mrs. Holcombe, we need to talk," said the suddenly appearing chief. I must have been day dreaming about Barry because I did not see the man arrive until he spoke to me.

"What about?" was my sullen response.

"That fourth man, have you figured out who that might be?"

"No sir, not yet. I may never know for sure."

The chief started to insert a key into the lock of my cell.

"Don't come in here!" I shouted as loud as I could.

"Mrs. Holcombe, calm down. I only want to talk to you."

"Stay out of here. I don't want you in here with me. I'll scream my head off and yell rape until someone comes running. Do you understand me, Chief?"

"That's fine. I will stay out and I do believe you have answered my question without my ever having asked it," he said as he walked away from my cell into the hall that led to the outer office and the chaos caused by the shift change.

"I want a lawyer!" I screamed into the building noise as the door was opened and he left the area.

CHAPTER 28: DON'T TELL THE CHIEF

I was the only person in a cell in this wing of the building. That definitely wasn't a good sign of what was to come. When breakfast was delivered I asked to speak to Barry Johnson as soon as he arrived. I also told the keeper of the keys, which this time was a lady of ample stature, that I wanted a lawyer.

I was alone all morning until the same keeper of the keys delivered my lunch consisting of chicken soup and a peanut butter sandwich.

"Ma'am," I said addressing my guard, "have you seen Barry Johnson?"

"He's off sick."

"I know. I was hoping he would check in. Can you get a message to him from me?"

"Why would I do that," she asked sarcastically.

"Tell him I know who the fourth man is. Also, tell him that the fourth man plans to kill me. Can you tell him that? Can you get that to him right away?"

"I'll ask the chief."

"No, please don't ask the chief. He doesn't like me and I'm afraid he will say something bad to the people that are going to charge me with the crimes. I'm not sure what crimes they are going to throw at me, but I don't want to make it any worse for myself. Please don't tell the chief?" I cried as I tried to persuade her to contact Barry. I knew that my life depended on it.

"I'll call Barry if he is out of the hospital. I'm not going to bother him if he is still in there."

"Fine, but please call him right away for me. I really need his help," I continued to plead and cry. The crying was the result of danger overload. Right at that moment, that was the only way my body could deal with everything that was happening to me.

The lady guard was gone and I was alone, again.

Not having slept the night before, made it almost impossible to keep my eyes open which I guess was a good thing. The chief wasn't going to do anything in broad daylight when so many people were around. He would want the deed to be done at night when a skeleton crew was on duty.

Barry didn't come.

Eddy didn't come.

Maggie didn't come.

I was so alone in the world. I vowed that once I got out of this mess, if I got out of this mess, I was going to be surrounded, at all times, by a multitude of friends and acquaintances. I was no longer going to follow the chosen path of being a loner.

It suddenly occurred to me that the chief might be blocking my friends and family from visiting me. That would explain why Eddy and Maggie hadn't appeared. What about Barry? Why hadn't he checked on me? He worked here. He had every right in the world to question me especially since he was helping me investigate in the first place.

Maybe the guard, I believe her name was May, didn't give him the message.

"Oh God, now what?"

The dinner tray was not very appetizing. I picked at the dry roast beef and ran the peas around the plate several times before I finally gave up and shoved the tray back through the slot to be picked up for return to the kitchen.

The silence of the evening was settling in and I was becoming more frightened with each passing minute.

It was midnight and once again the shift was changing.

I heard the door that entered the cell area open and close quietly. I knew I had a visitor.

"Ellen?"

"Barry? Is that you?"

"Are you okay, Ellen?"

"For now, I am. What's going on?"

"I'm waiting for the fourth man to show up?"

"You know who it is?"

"Yes, I do."

"I'm glad you're here."

"So am I."

Nothing more was said between Barry and me for what seemed like hours even though I know it was not that long.

We both waited and wondered when he was going to make his appearance and how he was planning to kill me.

I couldn't see Barry, he was well hidden.

The door opened and allowed foreign light to stream into the room from the outside. I saw the outline of the chief's body as he entered the room with a belt in his hand. It looked like the belt from my pant suit that they had taken away from me.

"Chief, are you planning to strangle me?" I asked as he moved briskly towards my cell.

"No, Mrs. Holcombe, you are going to hang yourself because of your remorse over everything that has happened to you."

"I haven't done anything for which I'm the least bit remorseful, Chief. Anybody that knows me would definitely know that. I'm not the suicide type. I would be more prone to commit murder than suicide."

"The way I see it, Ellen, I thinks it's about time I called you by your first name, don't you? Well, anyway, the way that I see it, is that you nearly caused the deaths of your son, your lover, and your best friend and her son. It was too much for your poor addled mind to withstand so you put an end to the pain. I think most everybody will believe that story."

"I don't think they will. I don't think my son will believe it. I know Barry won't believe it."

"If they pose problems at a later date, accidents will happen. You know how it is? Boys like your son get caught up on drugs, drinking, and speeding. Cops get killed quite often in the line of duty. Accidents can happen, Ellen. You know how it is these days."

"You can't kill everybody. Eventually someone will catch up with you and send you to the chair. You know you'll get the death penalty if you kill us all."

I was trying to keep him talking. I didn't know what Barry was planning to do to stop him, but I surely wanted to prolong his attack on me for as long as I could.

I knew the chief was running out of time. The flights to other countries, Cuba, Rio, and Mexico were scheduled for later this very day.

He and the lady police officer, Mary Smith, were leaving together headed for the same destination. I was sure of that.

Officer Roy Anderson and Detective Green probably were traveling together.

So-called Agents Thompson and Chandler would use the two remaining airline tickets.

That was the whole crew, I hoped and prayed.

"None of this would have been necessary if you all had kept your noses out of business that didn't concern any of you. If Maggie hadn't been out late at night and seen Thompson and Chandler coming out of the house; if her son hadn't gone looking for her and caught me going in and out of the green fence; if Barry had minded his own business; and if you had cared enough for your son to stay away; none of this would have happened."

"You're crazy, Chief. I did everything possible to keep my son out of this. You know that. You took him out of spite."

"Yes, I guess you're right. It kept you stirred up didn't it? I knew I would have to eliminate you eventually."

"But why?"

"Loose threads, I couldn't have any of those just lying around trying to wrap around someone's memory. I am afraid any type of thread that would connect this armored truck job to our little set up here at the Town of Stillwell Police Station might loosen a little each time the end is tugged until finally a slight pull completely unravels the chain. It's like when you tug on a thread on your shirt and end up opening up a seam with one simple little pull.

"You are a thread, Ellen. You have to be eliminated."

"What about the others? Won't they be able to put this all together?" I questioned as I tried to keep him talking.

"You are the only one who could really add up the whole problem and come to an answer."

"You said Maggie saw two of the men. Couldn't she identify them?"

"No, it was too dark but we didn't know that until we questioned her."

"So – I'm the only one that's actually slated for permanent and complete elimination?"

"Yes, unless they become problems at a later date. By that time, we will all probably be fanned out going in new directions to new and different lives."

He stepped forward and inserted the key into the lock.

I stepped back from the door as far into the cell as I could go.

"Help! Help me!" I screamed as he walked on into the cell with a confident swagger.

"Won't do any good to scream. There's no one out there. I sent them on wild goose chases all over the county. Unfortunately, there will be no one here to prevent you from hanging yourself because I am going to be called away for a dire emergency, if you know what I mean."

CHAPTER 29: I CLOSED MY EYES...

I closed my eyes and cowered down to the floor.

"Where are you, Barry," I screamed as I cringed in pure unadulterated fright.

"Right here and I have everything on this wire," he said as he stood over the chief's crumpled body.

"What did you do to him, Barry? Why is he down there?" I asked as I pointed to the chief's prone body.

"I used the butt of my gun on his hard head. I didn't want to kill him. I wanted the world to know what he has been doing to you."

"I haven't seen Eddy and Maggie. Are they all right?"

"Yeah, they're fine. The chief wouldn't let them in to see you. I guess he didn't want you to tell them anything that you know."

"How did you know I needed your help?"

"The message you gave to May to relay to me. I knew you were in trouble big time at that point. I had to find a way to help."

"Thanks, Barry, for believing in me."

ABOUT THE AUTHOR

Linda Hoagland has won acclaim for her mystery novels that include the recent *Snooping Can Be Doggone Deadly* and *Crooked Road Stalker.* She is also the author of works of nonfiction, a collection of short writings, along with a volume of poems. Hoagland has won numerous awards for her work including first place for the Pearl S. Buck Award for Social Change and the Sherwood Anderson Short Story Contest. She is currently the president of the Appalachian Authors Guild.

You can purchase Linda's work on her website:

lindasbooksandangels.com

See the list of her books on the

Linda Hudson Hoagland

following pages.

FICTION

The Backwards House

NONFICTION

Missing Sammy

90 Years and Still Going Strong

Quilted Memories

Living Life for Others

Watch Out For Eddy

Just a Country Boy: Don Dunford

The Little Old Lady Next Door (out of print)

COLLECTIONS

I Am... Linda Ellen

A Collection of Winners

ANTHOLOGIES

Broken Petals

Christmas Blooms